He looked. . .

Admit it, Kelly, sh[...] looks like a dream [...] walking around in a [...]

She stared into eyes the colour of an angry sea, trying to equal his dispassionate scrutiny, trying to convince herself that it was just the shock of seeing him again which made her heart thunder along like a steam train.

Dear Reader

We look at special care baby units with Josie Metcalfe's SECRETS TO KEEP, Caroline Anderson returns to the obstetrics unit—more babies—at the Audley Memorial in ANYONE CAN DREAM, while each heroine has a secret to keep from the hero. You will *love* William and Jacob!

We welcome back Sharon Wirdnam with CASUALTY OF PASSION, Meredith Webber's UNRULY HEART repatriates ill people and both books bring couples back together. A good month's reading!

The Editor

Sharon Wirdnam had a variety of jobs before training as a nurse and a medical secretary, and found that she enjoyed working in a caring environment. She was encouraged to write by her doctor husband after the birth of their two children, and much of her medical information comes from him, and from friends. She lives in Surrey where her husband is a G.P.

Recent titles by the same author:

SURGEON OF THE HEART
SEIZE THE DAY

CASUALTY
OF PASSION

BY

SHARON WIRDNAM

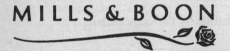

MILLS & BOON LIMITED
ETON HOUSE, 18–24 PARADISE ROAD
RICHMOND, SURREY, TW9 1SR

For the stars of Blood Transfusion—the great Vera
Hanwright, and in fond memory of Eleanor Lloyd.

*First published in Great Britain 1995
by Mills & Boon Limited*

© Sharon Wirdnam 1995

*Australian copyright 1995   Philippine copyright 1995
This edition 1995*

ISBN 0 263 78972 1

*Set in 10½ on 12½ pt Linotron Times
03-9502-48218*

*Typeset in Great Britain by Centracet, Cambridge
Made and printed in Great Britain*

CHAPTER ONE

'I TELL you, it was *him*— I actually *saw* him!'

Kelly heard the disbelieving sighs which followed this intriguing statement and wandered round into the female clinic room of St Christopher's world-famous accident and emergency department, her curiosity aroused.

She grinned at the three nurses huddled there. 'Sounds interesting. Saw who?'

Two of the student nurses looked to their undisputed leader, Staff Nurse Higgs—a statuesque blonde with magnificent smouldering blue eyes, who had given Kelly a particularly hard time since she'd arrived as casualty officer just a month earlier, since she didn't take kindly to what she obviously saw as competition. Now she shrugged her magnificent shoulders and stared at Kelly as though she had just met her for the first time. 'We're talking about the new surgical registrar,' she said reluctantly.

Kelly blinked. 'Oh? We have a new surgical registrar on the rotation every couple of years. What's so special about this one?'

Staff Nurse Higgs's bosom swelled with excitement. 'This one——' she paused for dramatic effect '—just happens to be a lord!'

Kelly quickly picked up an ampoule of penicillin that was sitting on a dressing trolley and pretended to study it as a tiny shiver iced her skin into goosebumps beneath the white coat she wore. 'A lord?' she queried carefully, noting objectively that her swallowing reflex seemed to have gone to pot.

'Mmm!' said Staff Nurse Higgs, almost licking her scarlet lips. 'Lord Rousay—a real member of the aristocracy! And that's not all—he's young, he's bloody gorgeous, *and*——' there was a dramatic pause '—he's single! What do you think about that?' Her eyes narrowed, her instinctive ability to sniff out gossip alerted. 'Are you OK, Dr Hartley— you've gone awfully pale?'

'Yes, of course I'm all right,' answered Kelly briskly. 'Why on earth shouldn't I be?'

'You've gone as white as a ghost—and look, your hand's trembling.' The eyes narrowed even further. 'You don't happen to *know* Lord Rousay, do you?'

No, I don't know him, thought Kelly bitterly. I thought I did, but I was young, foolish, naïve. I was just a nobody he tried to take advantage of. She shook her head, but not one strand of the dark auburn hair in its constricting chignon moved. 'Know him? Now, why would I know him?' she said brightly. 'There happen to be over twenty medical schools in the British Isles, with thousands of students, and while I know that lords in the medical world are pretty thin on the ground. . .' She paused for breath, her voice unusually high, and as she looked at their faces she realised that she was completely over-reacting. 'No, I don't know him,' she finished lamely, not caring that she lied.

At that moment, she was saved by the bell.

Literally. The sharp insistent peal of the red telephone on Sister's desk shrilled into their ears.

The emergency telephone: the one which never rang except in critical and life-threatening situations.

Nurse Higgs sped off, Lord Rousay temporarily forgotten, and Kelly followed her, her long and sleepless night shift banished by the rush of adrenalin which always accompanied a crisis. Life in the accident and emergency department was one long series of crises.

When she reached Sister's office, Nurse Higgs was just replacing the receiver. 'There's a child coming in,' she said succinctly. 'Aged two. Been savaged on face by a Rottweiler dog. Injuries extend to neck—the ambulance men are querying tissue damage to her airway. They're trying to intubate her, but there's swelling, apparently.'

'Bleep the duty anaesthetist,' said Kelly quickly. 'And can you send an experienced nurse into the resuscitation room to make sure the paediatric airway set is open? Did they say how bad the wound is?'

'No.'

'Well, when they arrive——' But Kelly's sentence was never finished because at that moment they heard the insistent sound of the ambulance's siren as it sped to the back entrance of the department.

'That's them!' said Kelly. 'Come on!'

Kelly ran out to greet it, Nurse Higgs hot on her heels. As soon as the back door was opened, Kelly climbed in, the blood draining from her face as she saw the extent of the child's injuries. No matter how experienced you were, it never left you—that feeling of helplessness when you saw someone who was terribly injured, especially when you were dealing with a toddler like this one.

The little girl was barely conscious. Shock, Kelly decided. Her breathing was stertorous but steady, and there was an airway *in situ*.

'We couldn't manage to intubate her,' said the driver, as he helped unhook the intravenous fluid bag from the drip stand before rushing the stretcher into A & E. 'You'll need an anaesthetist for that— the tissue is swollen.'

'He's on his way,' said Kelly briefly.

All the way into the department and along the short corridor to the resuscitation cubicle, she quizzed the drivers.

'What's her name?'

'Gemma Jenkins.'

Kelly bent her head and said softly into the child's ear, 'Hello, Gemma—I'm Dr Kelly. You're here in hospital and you're safe.'

Gemma remained unresponsive. Kelly turned worried eyes to the second ambulance man. 'When did this happen?'

'Only a few minutes ago, thank God.'

'Do we know how?'

The driver's mouth twisted with distaste. 'The dog belongs to the mother's boyfriend. He brought it round after a lunchtime session up the pub, rather the worse for wear. He disappeared into the bedroom with the mother, leaving the child to "play" with the dog.'

Kelly nodded. 'I see. Do we know where the mother is now?'

'She's following behind in a taxi. With the boyfriend.'

Kelly raised her eyebrows. 'But surely the mother wanted to accompany Gemma?'

'She's hysterical.'

'As well she might be,' said Kelly grimly.

'What she wanted,' said the ambulance driver, in the kind of weary voice which indicated that he had seen too much of the dross of life not to have become a cynic, 'was to comfort the boyfriend. He's worried that she'll press charges.'

Kelly, too, had grown used to the vagaries of human nature: these days she was rarely shocked, but this comment left her momentarily speechless. She shook her head in despair. 'Come on—let's get her on to the trolley.'

To Kelly's intense relief, the anaesthetist arrived and began to intubate the little girl. If he'd been delayed, Kelly could have done it at a pinch but, unless you'd had specialist training, trying to get an airway down a child's tiny trachea was notoriously difficult, particularly if the area was as swollen as this child's. The most common mistake was to insert the airway into the oesophagus instead of the trachea.

While the anaesthetist was extending the neck, Nurse Higgs began taking pulse, respiration and blood-pressure recordings, while Kelly gently wiped the blood away from Gemma's face so that she could see how bad the wound was.

It was bad enough. A great gaping gash which extended jaggedly down the left side of her face, but which had fortunately just missed the eye.

Kelly glanced up at the anaesthetist. 'How's her breathing?'

'Stable. And she's coming round.'

At least with the child's condition stabilised the danger of respiratory arrest had been allayed for the time being, thought Kelly, and she turned to Nurse Higgs. 'She needs suturing. Can you bleep the plastics surgeon?'

'The *plastics*?' queried Nurse Higgs, and the hostility which she had been showing towards Kelly since she had started three weeks ago finally bubbled over. 'Aren't you going to do it yourself?'

Kelly frowned with anger at the implied criticism. 'Nurse Higgs,' she said quietly, 'I'm adequate enough at stitching, but not arrogant enough to play God. I'm not sufficiently experienced to do delicate work of this nature—a botch-up here could cost a young child her looks and leave her with an unsightly scar. Now, are you going to bleep the plastics man for me, or am I going to have to do it myself?'

Nurse Higgs's eyes sparked malicious fire, but she bustled out without another word.

The anaesthetist raised an eyebrow. He was a tall, pale man, infinitely calm like most of his profession. 'Trouble?' he queried mildly.

'Nothing that I can't deal with,' Kelly answered resolutely, as she dipped another piece of cotton wool into the saline solution and very gently wiped some dried blood away.

'Report her,' he suggested.

Kelly shook her head. 'I'll manage,' she said, and dropped the used piece of cotton wool into the paper bag which hung on the side of the trolley.

They worked in silence, until the glimpse of a blinding white coat out of the corner of her eye told Kelly that the plastics man had arrived, but before she could get a proper look at him, she heard a horribly familiar laconic voice.

'I'm here to suture.'

Kelly looked up briefly, her eyes flicking to his name-badge. 'Randall Seton, Surgical Registrar'. His title, Lord Rousay—his still living father holding the title of Lord Seton, which Randall would one day inherit—was of course absent.

She swallowed, and looked down at the child again. 'I asked for someone from plastics,' she said. 'Not a general surgeon.'

He was already taking off his white coat and removing the gold cuff-links from his pristine pin-striped shirt. 'And there isn't anyone from plastics available,' he drawled, 'so you've got the next best thing. Me. Get me a pair of size nine gloves, would you, Staff?'

Staff Nurse Higgs had miraculously appeared by his side, like the genie from the lamp, and was staring up at him like an eager puppy. There was none of her delayed hearing problem in evidence today—the one which habitually had Kelly repeating her requests—and she sped off immediately to do the surgeon's bidding.

Kelly continued to clean the wound, her heart

racing. She was professional enough not to let him know how much his closeness bothered her, woman enough to be unable to deny the potency of his attraction.

'Right,' he murmured. 'Let's have some local anaesthetic drawn up, shall we, Staff?'

The voice was the same. Centuries of breeding, the finest schools, the big, country houses, privilege from the word go had guaranteed that Randall would speak with that confident, beautifully modulated English accent, as precise as cut glass. But it differed from the popular conception of the aristocratic voice, because it was deeper, sardonic, mocking—worlds away from the popular idea of the upper-class twit. It was an exquisite voice—smooth as syrup and dark as chocolate, the kind of voice which sent shivers down the spine of every woman from sixteen to ninety.

The wound was almost completely clean, and he had gloved up and was ready to start suturing.

'Thanks,' he said softly.

Their eyes met for a fraction of a second, and the impact of it was enough to make Kelly feel as though she had been winded and bruised by an unexpected blow.

'I'd better go and talk to the mother,' she said quickly, but he didn't seem to hear her. He was too busy pushing a fine syringe into the damaged area of the child's face with delicate precision even to notice Kelly's departure.

Heart hammering, Kelly picked up the casualty card, rang through to the reception desk, and asked for the mother of Gemma Jenkins to be sent along to the doctor's office.

She sat down, noticing dispassionately that her hands were actually trembling. She had never thought that she would see Randall ever again, she really hadn't—or perhaps that had been wishful thinking. But even given the notoriously closely knit world of British medicine, she certainly hadn't considered that just the merest glimpse of him, just the sound of that seductive mellifluous voice would be enough to shatter her composure and make her feel like the insecure seventeen-year-old she had been when she'd first met him.

She sighed. Nine long years ago. Where had they gone? Nine years of study, study, study and work, work, work.

And she had imagined that she had acquired a little sophistication on the way, had thought that she had become a little more worldly-wise. Was she going to let just the sight of Randall rip away all the complex layers of emotional maturity she had carefully constructed over the years?

Like hell she was!

There was a soft rap on the door, and Kelly instinctively sat upright in her chair, pulling her narrow shoulders back and arranging her features into a neutral expression.

'Come in!' she called.

Gemma's mother had, predictably, brought the boyfriend in, clinging possessively on to his arm, as though he were the first prize in a raffle. He had lurid tattoos over every available inch of flesh and he stank of booze. Kelly swallowed down the feeling of revulsion, determined to remain impartial. She had been taught, over and over again, that emotionally involved doctors who made value judgements were simply not doing their jobs properly.

The mother could have been little more than twenty-two—a woman who looked little more than a girl herself. She's younger than me, thought Kelly, with a jolt of surprise. And yet there was a grimy greyness to her complexion which told of a life lived inside, in high-rise blocks far away from the fresh air and the sunshine. She wore cheap, ill-fitting clothes. Her legs were pale and bare and she had squeezed her feet into tight, patent shoes, obviously new, though they were spattered with mud. On her heels she wore plasters where the shoes had obviously cut into her flesh. Her blonde hair was full of gel with little bits spiking upwards like a porcupine's, and already the dark roots were an inch long. Stooping, sad and pathetic, she stared back at Kelly with blank, disillusioned eyes and Kelly cursed a society which could allow the cycle of deprivation which had made this woman into one of life's losers. And would now probably do the same for her daughter.

She schooled her face into its listening expression. 'Mrs Jenkins?' she asked politely.

'It's *Miss*!' interrupted the man. 'That bastard didn't bother marrying her when she had his kid.'

'And your name is. . .?' prompted Kelly.

'Alan,' he swaggered. 'Alan Landers.'

'How's. . .how *is* Gemma?' the woman asked, her voice a plaintive whine.

At last. 'The doctor is suturing her face now,' said Kelly briskly. 'Given his skill, and the fact that your daughter is young enough to heal, well—we're hoping for the best, but I have to warn you that she *will* have a scar, though the surgeon is doing his best to ensure that it will be as small and as neat as possible.'

She took a deep breath. The police would investigate, but the A & E department themselves would need details of what had happened. 'Just for the record, would you mind telling me how it happened?'

Mr Landers screwed his face up into an ugly and menacing scowl. 'Stupid kid was winding the dog up. That dog wouldn't hurt no one.'

Refraining from pointing out the obvious flaw in his logic, Kelly thought that if she had been a man and not a doctor nothing would have given her greater pleasure than to punch this ignorant lout on the nose, but even if she *had* done, that wouldn't have been the answer. He had probably grown up fighting violence with violence, and as soon as he was old enough had gone out and bought an aggressive dog as a kind of ferocious status symbol, supposed to demonstrate just how much of a man he was.

Kelly looked directly at the man. 'Did you witness the attack?'

'Nah.'

'But it was your dog?' persisted Kelly, her fountain-pen flying as she wrote on the casualty card.

'That's right.'

'And you weren't there when it attacked?'

'That's right,' he said again.

Kelly had to bite back the incredulous question of how someone could leave a big, violent dog alone with a small child. 'So where were you when the attack took place on Gemma?'

This provoked a raucous belly laugh. 'In the bedroom,' he leered, and his eyebrows lifted suggestively as his gaze dropped to Kelly's breasts. 'Want me to tell you what we was up to?'

'That *won't* be necessary, Mr Landers,' said Kelly crisply. She turned to the woman and her totally vacant expression.

'You do know, Miss Jenkins, that I'm going to have to call in Social Services?'

'Do what?' The grey-faced woman was on her feet at once. 'And get some nosy-parker social worker sticking their oar in?'

Kelly looked at them both sadly. Didn't they realise that if the child was deemed to be at serious risk she could be taken away from them? God forgive her, but in a way she wished that Gemma *would* be free of them, if she hadn't also known that often children in care suffered from a different kind of neglect. 'I am also going to have to report the injury to the police——'

'What for?' the man demanded belligerently.

Kelly put her pen down. 'Because this category dog is supposed to be muzzled, Mr Landers—as I'm sure you know. It certainly shouldn't have been left alone in a room with a toddler. . .' Kelly paused, recognising that, despite all her pep-talking to herself, she had done the unforgivable—she *had* sounded judgemental. But doctors were human too, and she wondered seriously whether anyone in their right mind could have stopped themselves from adopting a critical tone with a case of this sort.

But it was when the man stabbed an angry finger in front of her face that she realised that if she wasn't careful, he really *could* turn nasty. She had better let him have his say. Even in her three short weeks in A & E, she had learnt that 'verbalising your feelings', as one of the social workers put it, also tended to defuse pent-up emotions.

Mr Landers's face was contorted into an ugly mask. 'You listen here to me, you little bitch——'

'What's going on in here?' came a deep, aristocratic drawl.

The three of them looked at the door, where the tall, dark and rangy form of Randall Seton stood surveying them through narrowed eyes.

The man replied in time-honoured fashion. 'Push off, you stuck-up git!'

There was a silence of about two seconds, and then Randall moved forward, his whole stance one of alert, healthy and muscular readiness. He radiated strength and he spoke with quietly chilling authority; but then, thought Kelly somewhat bitterly, that was the legacy of privilege too.

'Listen to me,' he said softly. 'And listen to me carefully. Dr Hartley has just been caring for your daughter in Casualty. So have I. I've just stitched together the most appalling wound inflicted by an animal that I've ever seen, praying as I did so that it will leave as little scar tissue as possible. An anaesthetist is currently pumping air down into her lungs, because where the dog's teeth ripped at her throat it caused such swelling that if an ambulance hadn't been on the scene so promptly, her airway could have been obstructed and your daughter could have died from lack of oxygen.'

The mother gave an audible gasp of horror, as though the reality of what had happened had just hit her.

'She is shortly going to be admitted to the children's ward,' he continued, 'where she will be looked after by another series of staff. Now we've all been doing our job, because that's what we're paid to do and that's what we chose to do. What we do *not* expect is to be criticised or insulted for doing just that. Have I made myself perfectly clear, Mr— Mr——?' The dark, elegent eyebrows were raised in query, but there was no disguising the dangerous spark of anger which made the grey eyes appear so flinty. At that moment, he looked positively *savage*, thought Kelly, but he somehow managed to do it in a very controlled kind of way. But there again, Randall was the master of self-control, wasn't he?

'Landers,' gulped the man. 'Yes, Doctor. I understand.'

'Good.' Then the dark-lashed grey eyes swept over Kelly. 'Can I see you for a minute?'

Nine years, she thought, slightly hysterically, and he asks can he see me for a minute. Breaking up with Randall—not that such a brief acquaintanceship really warranted such a grand-sounding title—had been the best thing which had ever happened to her. But she had often wondered, as women always did wonder about the first man who had made them dizzy with desire, just what would happen if they saw each other again. What would they think? What would they say?

She had never imagined such an inglorious reunion taking place in a tiny and scruffy little office in one of London's busiest A & E departments, nor him saying something as trite as that.

He looked. . .

Admit it, Kelly, she thought reluctantly. He looks like a dream. Every woman's fantasy walking around in a white coat.

He was lightly tanned. Naturally, he was tanned; he was always tanned. In the winter he skied down the blackest runs in Switzerland, and in the summer he holidayed with friends around the Mediterranean on a yacht which he had owned since the age of eighteen. Nine years hadn't added a single ounce of fat to that incredibly muscular body, honed to perfection by years of rigorous sport. The hair was as dark as ever, almost too black—a gypsy ancestor had been responsible for the midnight gleam of those rampant waves, he had once told her—sure!—and it curled and waved thickly around a neck which Michaelangelo would have died to sculpt.

She stared into eyes the colour of an angry sea, trying to equal his dispassionate scrutiny, trying to convince herself that it was just the shock of seeing him again which made her heart thunder along like a steam train. 'I can't,' she said. 'I'm afraid that I'm busy just now taking a history.'

He gave her a cool smile, the flash in the grey eyes mocking her. 'When you've finished, then?'

It would never occur to him to take no for an answer. 'I'm afraid that I may be tied up for some time.'

He shrugged the broad shoulders. 'In that case, I'll chase you up when I'm out of Theatre.' His eyes glittered. 'I can't wait.' It sounded awfully like a threat.

She wanted to say, Why bother? What was the point? Instead she shrugged her shoulders indifferently—a gesture which deserved to win her an Oscar. 'If you like,' she answered coolly. And picked up her pen again.

'And now, Miss Jenkins. If you'd like to give me a few more details. . .'

She didn't have time to think of him again during that shift; she was absolutely run off her feet. A middle-aged man came in on a stretcher with his leg badly broken in three places, and then a teenage girl was admitted with an overdose.

'How many has she taken?' Kelly asked her white-faced and trembling mother as she handed her the empty bottle.

'Only ten. That's all that was left in the box. She left a note. It said——' and here the woman started sobbing helplessly '—said it was to pay me back. I wouldn't let her go out last night, you see. Told her she had to revise for her exams, or she'd end up like me, Doctor, struggling just to survive.'

'Ssssh,' said Kelly softly, as she handed the sobbing woman a paper handkerchief. 'Try not to distress yourself.'

'She will be all right, won't she, Doctor?' asked the mother plaintively.

Kelly nodded, and answered with cautious optimism. 'I'm confident that she'll pull through. She's in good hands now.' Though it was lucky that the pills the girl had taken did not have any major side-effects.

She watched while the nurses, garbed in plastic gowns, gloves and wellington boots, put a wide tube into the girl's mouth and worked it down into her stomach. Then they tipped a saline solution into it, and waited for her to start retching. The physical ignominy of this uncomfortable procedure would hopefully make the girl think very carefully about attempting such an overdose again, Kelly hoped. Because what had started out as an angry gesture could have ended up with such tragic consequences.

She had been working in Accident and Emergency for just three weeks, but already she had discovered that her job was as much social worker as doctor—if she allowed it to be. And, frankly, she didn't have the time to allow it to be. The lives that people lived and the conditions in which they lived them sometimes made her despair, but there was little she could do to change anything, and accepting that had been a hard lesson.

It was seven o'clock by the time she finished, although she'd been due off at six. She had been held up with a cardiac arrest, and by the time she took her white coat off and washed her hands she was bushed, and could think of nothing she would like more than a hot bath, a good book, and an early night, particularly as she was not seeing Warren until tomorrow.

She set off for her room, through the winding corridors of St Christopher's—one of London's oldest and most revered hospitals. The main corridor was particularly impressive at night, and the ornately carved marble pillars dating back from a more prosperous time in the hospital's history cast long and intricate shadows on the well-worn stones of the floor.

Kelly heard a sound behind her. A sound she knew so well.

Sounds echoed on this particular floor and foot-steps were normal in a hospital. Day and night, people moved in endless motion.

But Kelly stiffened, then remonstrated silently with herself. Of course she wouldn't be able to recognise his footsteps. Not after nine years.

She turned round to face whoever was close behind her, as any sensible female doctor would.

And it was him.

'Hello, Kelly,' he said, his voice a deep, mocking caress, and Kelly felt herself thrill just to the sound of him speaking her name. He managed to make it sould like poetry, but he had always had the ability to do that.

And as she stared into eyes as silvery and as crystalline as mercury, nine years seemed just to slip away, like grains of sand running through her fingers.

CHAPTER TWO

NINE summers ago Kelly had been in the first year of her school's sixth form, studying science, and studying hard. When other students moaned about the rigorous demands of the syllabus they were expected to cover, Kelly did not. Her study had been hard fought for.

Not many students had to fight their parents to stay on at school—it was often the other way round—but Kelly's parents simply had not been able to understand why she didn't want to leave school at the earliest opportunity to start 'bringing a bit of money in', as they put it. Which, loosely translated, meant—certainly in the culture which Kelly had grown up in—to help boost her mother's already meagre income, made even more meagre by her father's liking for a drink and a bet on the horses. What they had expected for Kelly was a local shop or factory job. But Kelly refused to be condemned to a life of drudgery before getting married to a man like her father and having to scrimp and save and hide her money from him.

Kelly had tried to hide her bitterness at the lack of ambition in the Hartley household, knowing that any hint of rebellion would seal her fate. And she was lucky in two respects. The first was that she had been born with an outstanding intellect, and the second was that she had an absolute champion in her chemistry teacher—a Mr Rolls. Not only did his passion for his subject inspire her to work as hard as she possibly could, but through him she learned really to love the discipline of science.

If Mr Rolls had never achieved his full potential, he was determined that Kelly should not follow the same pattern. In his late thirties, he had never married, instead devoting all his energies to his students. It was Mr Rolls who spoke to Kelly's dazed parents, told them that it would be a crime if she were not allowed to pursue higher education. It was he who allayed their financial fears by telling them that all sorts of grants were available for gifted students these days, and that they would not be asked to provide money they simply did not have. The only thing he did not discuss with them, at Kelly's behest, was her ambition to become a doctor.

'Time enough for that,' Kelly told him firmly.

'But why?' He was genuinely non-comprehending.

She stared back at him, her large green eyes already wise beyond their years, in so many ways. 'Because it will honestly be too much for them to take in all at once,' she told him gently. 'To tell them that I want to become a doctor would be like telling them that I want to fly to Venus!'

But she had felt as though if she spread her arms she really *could* fly to Venus that August evening, as she walked up the gravelled drive of the enormous country house for the summer school in science which Mr Rolls had insisted she attend. He had even arranged for the school governors to sponsor the trip.

'And Seton House is in the heart of the country,' he told her smilingly. 'Do you good to get out of London for a bit—put a bit of colour in your cheeks.'

Kelly had never seen such a beautiful place in all her life as Seton House. It was not *quite* as impressive as Hampton Court Palace, which she had visted on a trip with the Brownies years ago, but it came a pretty close second, with its sweeping manicured lawns in the most dazzling shade of emerald, and its carefully clipped yew trees, and its parklands.

She stared up at the house, slightly fearful of knocking, when at that moment the vast door opened and a man in his early twenties came running lightly down the steps, saw her, stopped, and smiled. He had thick, black hair and the longest pair of legs she had ever seen.

'Well, *hello!*' His eyes were sparkling—fine grey eyes with exceptionally long black lashes—as they looked Kelly up and down with open appreciation.

That summer she had grown used to the stares from men; it had been a liberating summer in more ways than one. She had grown her hair, so that it rippled in dark red waves all the way down her back, and the faded jeans and T-shirt which every student wore emphasised the slim curve of her hips, the gentle swell of her burgeoning breasts. If men ogled her, she soon put them in their place. But somehow she didn't mind this man looking one bit. It gave her the chance to look at him, and he was, without exception, the most delectable man she had ever set eyes on. 'Hello,' she answered. 'Who are you?'

He grinned. 'Well, actually I'm wearing two hats this week.'

Kelly blinked. 'Excuse me? Your head is bare.'

His eyes narrowed, and he laughed—the richest, deepest, most mesmerising sound she could imagine. 'Sorry. What I mean is that I'm one of the medical students running the course, and I. . .' And then his gaze fell to the cheap and battered old suitcase she was clutching, and his eyes softened. 'Come inside. You must be tired after your journey. Here, let me carry your bags for you,' and he took them from her without waiting for her assent. 'Come with me. I'll show you to your room. You're the first to arrive. We weren't expecting anyone until this evening.'

'I—caught the early train,' faltered Kelly, as she followed him up the steps leading to the house. The cheaper train, the bargain ticket, planning to kill time looking around the village of Little Merton. Except that when she had arrived in Little Merton there had been absolutely nothing to see, so she had come straight on up to the house. 'I can always go away and come back later,' she ventured.

'What to do? There's not a lot to see in Little Merton!'

'So I noticed,' remarked Kelly drily, and he turned his head to stare down at her again, giving her another of those slow smiles. She wondered if he knew just how attractive those smiles were—he *must* do!

Kelly followed him into the vast entrance hall,

with him still holding her bags. No one had ever carried her bags for her before; in her world, women struggled with the heavy items, like pack-horses for the most part. She rather liked this show of masculine strength, and of courtesy. It made her feel fragile and protected, and rather cherished.

She stared around the hall. She had never imagined that a place could be so large and so beautiful, without being in the least bit ostentatious. There was none of the over-the-top gold scrolling which had abounded in Hampton Court. Instead, just an air of quiet loveliness, and the sensation of continuity down through the ages, of treasures being treasured and passed on for the next generation to enjoy.

'It's quite perfect,' said Kelly simply.

He looked down at her. 'Isn't it?' he said quietly. 'I'm glad you like it.'

It didn't occur to her to ask why. She just assumed that, like her, he had an eye for beautiful things.

He showed her upstairs to her room, decorated in a striking shade of yellow with soft sage-green fittings. It was just like being at the centre of a daffodil, thought Kelly fancifully.

'It's rather small, I'm afraid,' he apologised. 'But we've put some of the boys in the larger rooms, sharing.'

Small? Kelly gulped. It was palatial! She had spent the last fifteen years sharing a shoe-box of a room with a sister whose idea of tidying up was to chuck all the mess into an already overflowing cupboard! 'It's lovely,' she told him, wandering over to the window. 'And oh——' her gaze was suddenly arrested by the tantalising glitter of sunlight on water in the distance '—is that a lake I can see?'

'Mmm.' He came to stand beside her. 'We have black swans nesting there. Very rare and very beautiful. I'll show you later if you like.'

'I'd like that very much.'

He smiled.

She was suddenly very conscious of just how tall he was, how broad his shoulders; aware too of the powerful thrust of his thighs, similarly clad in denim more faded than her own jeans. She wasn't used to being alone in bedrooms with strange men, she thought, her heart beating hard, but he seemed unconcerned by his surroundings. But then, why should he not be? He was a medical student, and about twenty-four, she guessed. He would not look twice at a seventeen-year-old schoolgirl.

All the same, she felt that it was probably wise to establish a more formal footing.

'Which medical school are you at?' she enquired politely.

'St Jude's. I'm in my final year. How about you?'

'Another year of A-levels, then I'm hoping to get a place at St Christopher's.'

He frowned. 'So you're—how old?'

'Seventeen— *just!*' she smiled, disconcerted to see an expression of disquiet pass over his features. 'There's nothing wrong, is there?'

He shook his head. 'I somehow thought that you were older than that. Most of the students here are just about to go up to medical school. Some are even in their first year. You must be very good to be here.' The grey eyes were questioning.

Kelly smiled, not falling into the trap of false modesty, knowing her own worth and ability as a student. 'You'll have to be the judge of that,' she answered coolly.

Their eyes met, his giving a brief but unmistakably appreciative flash, and she found that she could not look away, that his face seemed to be at the centre of her whole universe right at that moment. She became aware of other things too, things that up until now she had only read about in biology textbooks: the sudden drying of her mouth and the hammering of her heart. The tightening of her breasts, as though they had become heavy and engorged with blood. And the sudden rucking of her nipples—exquisite and painful and highly disturbing.

Kelly wasn't stupid. She had grown up in a neighbourhood where girls experimented sexually with boys from as early an age as fourteen, and up until now she had always been disapproving and highly critical of such behaviour. Now, for the first time in her life, she acknowledged the dangerous and potent power of sexual attraction.

She turned away, wondering if he had seen the betraying signs of that attraction in her body. 'I'd better unpack,' she said awkwardly. 'Thanks for showing me to my room. . .' She hesitated. 'I don't even know your name.'

He paused for a moment before answering. 'It's Randall,' he told her. 'And yours?'

'Kelly. Kelly Hartley.'

'Because your eyes are Kelly-green?' he hazarded.

She shook her head and laughed. 'My mother says I was named after Grace Kelly, but my father disagrees. He says it was Ned Kelly—the bandit!'

He laughed too, then stayed her with a light touch of his hand on her forearm as she moved towards the tatty suitcase which looked ridiculously out of place amidst the restrained elegance of the room. 'Don't unpack now—there'll be plenty of time for that later. It's such a glorious day. Why don't you let me show you something of the countryside? We could have lunch somewhere. That's if you'd like to?'

She would like to very much, although the sensible, studious Kelly could think of all kinds of reasons why she shouldn't go gallivanting off to lunch with someone she had barely met. But something in the soft silver-grey of his eyes was proving to be impossibly enticing. He was not the first man to have asked her out, but he was the first one she had ever said yes to.

She grinned. 'I'd love to. Do I need to change?'

He shook his head. 'You look fantastic. Do you have a ribbon or something?'

Kelly nodded. 'Why?'

'Bring it, you'll need it.'

The reason why was a small, gleaming scarlet sports car which was garaged in an area he called the 'old stables'. Kelly's eyes widened. Brought up with frugality as her middle name, she said the first thing which came into her head.

'How on earth can you afford a car like this as a student?'

He seemed surprised by her frankness. 'It was a twenty-first birthday present,' he told her as he opened the car door for her. 'From my parents.'

'Generous parents,' commented Kelly wryly, as she climbed into the car.

He moved into the seat next to her, and turned the ignition key. 'Oh, they're certainly generous,' he said, in a voice which sounded strangely bitter. 'That's to say, they find it very easy to buy things.'

She stole a glance at him. 'What's wrong with them buying things?'

The silver-grey eyes were direct; disburbing. He shrugged. 'It doesn't make up for them never having been there, I suppose.'

'Doesn't it? I have exactly the opposite problem with my parents,' answered Kelly, giving a rueful little smile, wondering if anyone was ever contented with their lot.

'Then I guess we'll just have to comfort one another, won't we?' he said, his voice soft, mocking, having the power to increase her pulse-rate just with its deep, velvety caress.

Suddenly shy, Kelly quickly gathered her thick red hair up in the black velvet ribbon, afraid he might notice that she was blushing like crazy.

He turned on the ignition, and the little car roared off down the drive, spitting out pieces of gravel in its wake, and Kelly sat back in the seat to enjoy the drive.

It was one of those afternoons which stayed in the memory forever—the most perfect afternoon of Kelly's life. He drove her to a country pub for lunch where they ate crusty bread and great slabs of farmhouse cheese, washed down with local beer. After that, they walked. And talked. They didn't seem to stop talking. She told him all about the tiny terraced house she had grown up in, about the shared bedroom and the thin walls where the neighbours' arguments were broadcast so loudly that they might have been in the same room. She told him of her burning ambition to be a surgeon, and his eyes had narrowed.

'It's tough enough, anyway,' he observed. 'Even tougher for a woman.'

'I know,' she said passionately. 'And I don't *care*! I'm going to defeat all the odds, you wait and see!'

He had smiled then, his eyes soft. 'I can't wait,' he murmured.

She blushed again, realising that she had been monopolising the conversation; he was so incredibly easy to talk to. 'Now tell me about you,' she urged him.

'What, everything?' he teased.

'Absolutely *everything*!'

And Randall painted a picture of his own world, so very different from hers. Kelly's heart turned over when he described being sent away to boarding school at the tender age of eight.

'Cold showers and cross-country runs,' he said, and shuddered theatrically.

'Did you really hate it?' she asked sympathetically.

'I *loathed* it,' he said with feeling, then grinned. 'Don't look so tragic, Kelly—it was a long time ago,' and he took her hand in his. She didn't object; her head was spinning, as though he had intoxicated her just with his presence.

The afternoon flew by and it was almost six when they arrived back at the house. There were several cars parked in front of the house, and a woman, small and matronly, stood on the steps, talking to a group of people, most slightly older than Kelly, and whom she assumed were other medical students.

When the little sports car came to a halt, the woman came hurrying over to them, barely looking at Kelly, her face reproving. '*There* you are, my lord!' she exclaimed. 'Everyone's been looking for you. Five medical students and no one knows where to put them.'

Kelly stiffened. *Lord*!

'Calm down, Mary,' he drawled in a voice born to giving orders, and Kelly watched while the older woman softened under the sheer potency of all that charm. 'I'll sort it out. Mary—I'd like you to meet Kelly Hartley. Kelly—this is Mary. She lives here and provides food to die for.'

But Kelly knew instantly from his proprietorial tone that Mary 'lived' here purely in the capacity of staff. She felt somehow betrayed. They had shared intimacies, swopped secrets—and yet he had left out something as fundamental as the fact that he was a member of the flaming aristocracy! Her cheeks were hot with anger, but she managed to keep her voice relatively calm. 'Thank you very much for lunch,' she said crisply. 'I'll leave you to it—you're obviously terribly busy.'

'Kelly——' he began, but Kelly had jumped out of the car and run past the staring group and upstairs to her room before he could say anything more, or stop her.

And when the peremptory knock came on her door about half an hour later, she was not surprised, though she was tempted not to answer it.

She pulled the door open to find Randall leaning with languid grace against the door-frame, his grey eyes narrowed. 'Why are you angry?' he asked calmly.

'Why do you think?'

'If I knew that, I wouldn't be asking.'

'Why on earth didn't you tell me that you were a lord?' she demanded.

'Oh, that,' he said casually.

'Yes, *that*!' she retorted. 'I suppose that you actually *own* this house too?'

He shrugged. 'Guilty as charged. Although on a technical point, I won't actually own it until my father dies.'

'Damn you and your technical point!' she fired back. 'Why didn't you tell me?'

He came inside, closed the door firmly behind him and took her by the shoulders. 'Because I didn't want you to know. Not then.'

Kelly's eyes widened. 'Why ever not?'

'Because people can be intimidated by the title, and I suspected that you might be one of them.'

She took a step back. 'Why, of all the most *patronising*——'

'And because sometimes the baggage which comes with all that stuff,' he interrupted coolly, 'just gets in the way of what really matters. . .you know?'

She shook her head, angry and confused. 'No, I don't know.'

'Yes, you do,' he said softly, and bent his head to kiss her. 'Of course you do.'

After that Kelly spent every moment she could with him, and for the first time in her life found it difficult to concentrate on her studies. He had put her in his tutorial group, and she really had to make an effort not to run her gaze dreamily over every glorious inch of his body, and to listen instead to his lectures, which she wasn't at all surprised to discover were absolutely brilliant.

Randall was the undisputed star of the course, and it was pretty obvious that every girl fancied him like mad, but he seemed to have eyes only for Kelly. At the end of each day's session he would take her off somewhere in his little sports car and they would walk for miles, arriving back only just in time for dinner.

'Should you be leaving them alone like this?' Kelly asked him, as the little sports car came to a halt and she tried to drag the brush through her tangled hair.

He smiled. 'Relax. There's plenty for them to

do—I'm not playing nanny to them. Now come here
and kiss me before we go inside.'

Kelly was quite certain that she was in love with
him. But it was more than just the completely
overwhelming physical attraction she had been
aware of from the very beginning, because he gave
her a great sense of her own worth for her intellect,
as well as a woman.

Thoughts of him disturbed her nights, and she
tossed restlessly as she relived how his amazing grey
eyes would darken with passion every time he took
her into his arms. She suspected that she would
willingly have gone to bed with him, except that he
behaved with a restraint which she found admirable,
given that even with her total inexperience she
recognised just how much he wanted her.

And then came that last evening.

First there was dinner, cooked as usual by Mary,
and then someone had laughingly suggested cha-
rades. So they all filed into the room which was
known as the red library, but after a time Randall
took her by the hand and led her quietly from the
room. She didn't know whether anyone noticed that
they had left, and, aware that she was leaving the
following day, she no longer cared. Silently she went
up the staircase with him, her heart beating like a
wild thing when he led her straight to her bedroom
and closed the door quietly behind them.

He stared at her for a long, long moment. 'I'm
going to miss you, Kelly,' he said softly. 'Very,
very much.'

She could have drowned in the intensity of that silver-grey stare. 'Are you?' she whispered.

'More than you could ever imagine.' He took her into his arms, his face dark and unreadable, the light from the moon emphasising the aristocratic cheekbones, the sculptured perfection of his mouth. He bent his face so that it was very close to hers. 'And I want to see you again—you know that, don't you?'

Kelly nodded silently, shaken by the fervour in his voice, which matched some spark deep in her soul. She wound her arms around his neck, and her body seemed to melt into the hard sinews of his, her unspoken surrender apparent in the kiss she returned so sweetly.

He gave a low moan as he ran his hands through the thick, silken texture of her hair, then let them fall to her waist, to gather her in even closer, so that they were moulded together and she never wanted to let him go. Never, never, never.

Her breasts tingled as he stroked them over the cotton of the simple white dress she wore, and she gave a little sigh, her eyes closing as she felt the warm river of desire flood her veins with sweet potency.

Still kissing her, he slid the zip of her dress down and she let her arms drop to her sides so that it glided down over her hips and pooled on the ground around her feet. He raised his head then, his eyes narrowed as they studied her. Her breasts were so small that she wore no bra, and she was clad only in the smallest pair of bikini briefs, her body silvered by the pale light of the moon, the thick waves of her hair tumbling down over her small, high breasts. Suffused with love and longing for him, Kelly felt exultant as she saw the expression on his face as his gaze slowly covered every inch of her, filled with an elemental and very feminine fire as she revelled in the power of her body, that *she* could inspire that look of ardour on his face.

'You're so beautiful,' he told her. His voice sounded unsteady, almost slurred with desire, as he started to unbutton his shirt, letting it fall to the ground as carelessly as her dress had done.

'So are you,' she whispered, and she heard him give a low laugh as his hand moved to the belt of his trousers.

Kelly felt shy at her first sight of his arousal, almost dazed and daunted by her ability to do that to him, but her shyness evaporated as he slid her tiny bikini pants down over her thighs, then, naked, pulled her down on to the bed with him and began to kiss her over and over again.

It felt so good. It felt so right. She was drowning in delight, each touch and each kiss making the pleasure escalate until she could hardly bear it any more, almost going out of her mind when his hand moved over the flatness of her belly, to teasingly stroke tiny provocative circles there. She began to move restlessly, and he gave another low laugh as his hand slid down between her thighs to tantalise her even further so that she made an instinctive little pleading sound at the back of her throat.

'Do you want me?' he whispered huskily.

'Oh, yes,' she shuddered ecstatically as he stroked her skilfully.

'Really want me?'

'Yes!' Oh, God, yes—more than she had ever wanted anything in her entire life.

He moved to lie on top of her. She was ready for him, gloriously and deliciously ready for him; ripe and hot and moist. She pressed her lips to his shoulders, eager for him to fill her, thrilling as he gently parted her legs, when a stark and elemental fear pierced through the mists of her desire with frightening clarity, as the dreaded phrase of her childhood came back to mock at her.

'That girl's in trouble.'

In trouble. . .

Kelly remembered Jo Grant at school, only fifteen, but now prematurely aged as she pushed the pram up the hill every morning.

'Randall,' she whispered urgently.

He lifted his head from her breast, his voice thick with passion. 'What?'

'You won't——'

'Oh, I most certainly will, my darling,' he murmured.

'—make me pregnant, will you?'

The silence which filled the room was brittle, electric. She felt him tense, heard him stifle some profanity, before he rolled off her, and, with his back to her, the broad set of his shoulders forbidding and stiff with some kind of unbearable tension, began to pull his clothes on.

Kelly was filled with hurt and confusion. She had
meant. . .had meant. . .that they should. . .

'Randall?' she whispered tentatively, and when he
turned, in the act of wincing as he struggled to zip
up his trousers, she almost recoiled from the look of
frustration on his face, which quickly gave way to
one of bored disdain.

'You certainly pick your moments,' he drawled
cuttingly. 'Couldn't you have said something
earlier?'

'Well, what about you?' Outraged and indignant,
she sat up, her hair tumbling to conceal her breasts,
and she saw a nerve begin to work in his cheek.
'You didn't seem inclined to discuss it either. Don't
you think that you have some responsibility too?'
she demanded.

'That's just the trouble, Kelly,' he said, in a bitter,
flat and angry voice. 'I wasn't doing any thinking at
all.'

And without another word he slammed his way
out of the room, leaving Kelly to spend the most
miserable night of her life.

The next morning she had risen early, hoping to
get away before anyone else was up, and yet trying
to suppress the foolish and humiliating little hope
that he would still want to see her. She quickly
packed her few belongings into the suitcase and went
silently down the stairs.

Mary was placing a pile of newspapers on a tray,
and looked up, her eyes hardening with disapproval
when she saw Kelly.

'Will you be wanting breakfast, miss?' she asked grudgingly.

Kelly shook her head. 'No, thank you. I—I'd like to get away just as soon as possible. Will you please——' she swallowed. She must be courteous; she still had her pride '—thank Randall for his hospitality?'

'Yes, miss. Though I don't know when I shall be seeing him next.'

'I'm sorry? But he'll be down for breakfast before he goes back, surely?'

'Oh, *no*, miss.'

Kelly's heart started thundering with the implication behind the cook's triumphant statement.

'Just that Lord Rousay's already gone back to London. Left here at dawn, he did. Driving that car of his as though the devil himself was chasing him.'

'Oh, I see,' said Kelly, in a small, empty little voice, as the fairy-tale disintegrated.

And she had never set eyes on him again.

CHAPTER THREE

UNTIL now.

Kelly stared at Randall, her features schooled into the coolly indifferent look she had perfected over the years because that passionate and impetuous creature who had offered herself so willingly to Randall Seton had gone forever.

'You've gone very pale—you look as though you could use a drink,' he observed. 'Let me buy you one.'

Kelly almost exploded with rage. Did he imagine—did he have the termerity to imagine—that he could simply walk into her life nine years on and calmly ask her for a drink, and that she, panting eagerly, would accept? 'No, thank you,' she answered, her voice iced with pure frost.

He was blocking her path. 'Kelly—this is crazy. We need to talk.'

She frowned, looking perplexed. 'Do we? I can't think why.'

'Because we go back a long way. Don't we?' He smiled, so sure of its effect, so sure that the grin which creased his handsome features would have her eating out of his hand.

'Hardly,' she murmured. 'We were little more than acquaintances a long time ago. Let me see—it must be eight years, surely—or was it seven? I can hardly remember.'

'Nine,' he gritted, and then a wry and reluctant look of amusement spread over his features. 'OK, Kelly—you've made your point with stunning effect, but I still want to talk to you, and I don't particularly want to do it in this draughty corridor. Not when I can think of so many more attractive venues.'

'I'm *sure* you can,' she bit out crisply. 'But the fact remains that I really can't be bothered talking to you. I've had a busy day and I'm very tired. What I want is a bath and an early night. Now have you got that, Randall—or would you like me to spell it out in words of one syllable for you?'

He carried his assurance like a badge, and Kelly realised with a gleeful feeling that he was finding it very difficult to cope with her refusal. She would lay a bet that he had never had to cope with rejection in his charmed life. A look of frustration crossed over his face, to be quickly replaced by one of narrow-eyed perception, and Kelly wondered whether she had gone just a bit overboard on her hostility towards him.

Because he wasn't stupid. Far from it. He could probably put two and two together and come up with another theory of relativity. If she carried on sniping quite so vehemently, might he not guess that he had broken her heart, hurt her so much that she had vowed never to let a man get so close to her again?

She sighed. Indifference was a far better shield to hide behind than anger. Anger symbolised emotion, and she had buried emotion a long time ago. She glanced down at the slim gold watch on her wrist.

'Sorry.' She stifled a yawn, and gave him a polite little smile. 'I'm just very tired, that's all.'

'Then you need a drink,' he said firmly. 'Where would you like to go? There's a bar in the mess, isn't there?'

Kelly bit her lip. That was the last thing she wanted, to be seen with him in the doctors' mess. Hospitals were a hot-bed of gossip, and word would be bound to get back to Warren if she was seen out with the hospital's newest and most eligible bachelor.

'Yes, there is,' she answered grudgingly. But since the alternative would be to offer him a drink in her room, and she certainly was not going to do that, there seemed to be nothing to do except give in gracefully. 'OK,' she shrugged. 'But just a quick drink.'

He knew the way to the mess. They walked in silence along the echoing floors, and Kelly was reminded of just how tall he was, and how striking, since every nurse they passed looked him up and down with blatant appreciation.

The doctors' mess was a largish room, built on the lines of a pub, though the prices were subsidised. It was only half filled, with small groups of doctors, and the occasional table of nurses. Kelly's heart sank as she spotted Staff Nurse Higgs chewing at a cherry on a stick, the movement frozen when she spotted Randall, her blue eyes widening, and then a frown knitting her arched brows together as her gaze

alighted on Kelly by his side. I might as well have
taken a full-page advertisement out, thought Kelly
on a sigh, as she followed Randall over to an
unoccupied table.

'What would you like?' he asked.

'Any kind of juice, thanks.'

He raised his eyebrows. 'You don't drink?'

'Of course I do, but only in the right company,'
she replied sweetly, and his mouth twisted in anger
as he turned away from her and made his way to the
bar.

He returned, carrying two tall tumblers of pine-
apple juice and a saucer of black olives.

He sat down opposite her and his grey eyes
regarded her steadily.

Under that cool appraisal, Kelly was hard put to
find something neutral to say. 'You're not drinking
either?' she queried.

He shook his head, took an olive and bit into it.
'I'm on call tonight. A young lady I operated on this
afternoon may need to go back to Theatre, and I've
a very sick patient in Intensive Care. It's a busy
rota.'

'So I believe.' Under the cover of picking up her
glass and sipping at the juice, Kelly was able to
observe him surreptitiously from beneath her long
lashes. She had thought that he hadn't changed but,
close to, of course he had changed. She saw tiny
lines which fanned at the side of his amazing grey
eyes and they had not been there nine years ago.
His face was leaner too—it had lost that youthful
fullness. He had been twenty-four when she had first

met him, and he had to be—good grief, she thought—he would be almost thirty-three now. Her eyes strayed to his hands.

'No, I'm not married.' A mocking voice disturbed her thoughts.

Kelly froze. She gave him a steady stare. 'I *beg* your pardon?'

He looked completely unrepentant. 'That's what you wanted to know, wasn't it?' The grey eyes swept over her own bare hands. 'And neither are you, I see. Married, that is.'

Kelly looked at him with dislike. 'How you do jump to assumptions, Randall,' she said, in her most chilly voice. 'Lots of women copy men and don't bother to wear wedding-rings these days.'

'And are you one of those women?' he asked softly.

There was a pause. 'As a matter of fact, I'm not married. Although I fail to see what business it is of yours?'

'Do you?' he mocked, imitating the stilted tone of her voice, then leaned back in his chair to study her. 'You've changed,' he said suddenly.

If he started reminiscing—if somehow he had the ability to remind her of the glorious week they had shared, the memory of which even its inglorious ending could not destroy—then she would be lost. And vulnerable. And she had vowed never to be that vulnerable again.

She gave a brittle little laugh. 'Well, of course I've changed, Randall,' she said, rather in the manner in which a schoolmistress might scold a child. 'What did you expect, that I would stay exactly the same person?'

'I rather wish you had,' he said quietly. 'There's a restraint about you now, a brittleness which is totally at odds with the girl I once knew.'

Kelly put her glass down on the table with such force that a group of doctors and nurses on the other side of the mess turned to look at her curiously, but she didn't care—she was past caring. 'How dare you invite me for a drink and start insulting me? And how dare you speak with such authority about my character, when you don't even know me—and *you never did*?'

'Didn't I?' he mocked. 'I'd say I knew you pretty——'

She interrupted him before he could utter a word as damning as 'intimately' and have her face burning shamefully with the memory. 'Well, you're wrong!' she bit back vehemently. 'I was just a little carried away that week—it obviously went to my head,' and she slipped into a brilliant parody of a cockney accent, 'to have his lordship take notice of a humble little schoolgirl. . .'

She didn't know whether it was the dart about her youth or about his title which caused that tight look of rage to twist his mouth into an ugly line, but she was glad, yes, *glad*. If she could cause Randall Seton even a moment's discomfort, then so be it—for it wouldn't cause him an iota of the pain he had caused her. She got to her feet and stared down at him. 'I knew that this drink would be a bad idea. You should have listened to me. Goodbye, Randall.' And she walked swiftly from the mess, aware of curious eyes on her, realising that their voices must have been raised and knowing that news of their little contretemps would be all round the hospital by lunchtime tomorrow.

It was when she was unlocking the door to her room that she realised he had followed her, and she turned to find him behind her, hearing the quickened sound of his breathing and seeing the look of anger which distorted the exquisite features. And still she did not have the sense to leave well alone.

'Still here?' she queried insultingly. She raised her eyebrows. 'Tell me, Randall, did you enjoy it so much—*slumming* it with me? Is that why you won't go away and leave me alone?'

And then she knew she had gone that little bit too far, as she saw the broad set of his body tense up as though for fight. The anger had all but disappeared, leaving a cold and cruel mask in its place, and Kelly knew a little shudder of apprehension. 'You little bitch,' he said softly, and his mouth swooped down to claim hers in a harsh and heavenly kiss which was just stamped with sexual domination.

As his mouth began a hot and erotic penetration, Kelly almost swooned against the open door, and she might have fallen had his arm not gone out to encircle her slender waist in a steely grip. He pushed her inside the room, his mouth plundering hers with a sweetly rapacious invasion all the time, and Kelly felt her breasts tingle into life, uncaring that he had pushed her against the wall, and that his hips were moulded into hers, demonstrating with sweet and daunting clarity the measure of his arousal. She felt his hand push her white coat away from her breasts, before he lightly brushed the palm of his hand over each aching and tumescent peak, and Kelly held on to him tightly, her eyes closed helplessly, a small cry of frustration and pleasure torn from her lips. And sorrow, too—that only Randall could do this to her. She fought to catch her breath, fought for control, and he released her mouth then, leaving her bereft and longing for the taste of him again.

'Such a pity to have to tie all that glorious hair back,' he observed, as his grey eyes lazily surveyed the stark hairstyle she had adopted for work. And she heard the amusement in his voice. A hateful, mocking amusement.

His hand moved before she could stop it, and he had deftly removed all the pins at the nape of her neck, so that the rich, dark red waves tumbled down around her face. Over her shoulder she caught a glimpse of herself—the green of her eyes almost completely obscured by the black, glittering pupils, her mouth all red and pouting and swollen from the pressure of that kiss which had seemed to go on and on, and yet be over far too quickly. But it was the hair which really seemed to symbolise her surrender. Cascading unusually all over her snowy white coat, she looked nothing more nor less than a wanton. A wild and sensual creature.

Lips trembling, she turned to him. 'Get out of here,' she said on a whisper.

'Quite sure?' he mocked her. 'I can stay if you

want me to. The pleasure would be—my oh, so responsive Kelly—all mine.'

'Either you get out now or I slap your arrogant face.'

He grinned devilishly. 'Kelly, *darling*,' he drawled arrogantly, 'you've become so *aggressive*.'

Summoning a deep, deep breath, Kelly marched over to the other side of the room, where the old-fashioned black telephone sat. 'Or,' she said calmly, 'I can ring the authorities and tell them——'

'Tell them what?' he interrupted. 'Tell them that I kissed you, and you kissed me back? That if I hadn't stopped we'd be lying in that bed now, doing what we should have done all those years ago?'

Kelly lifted the receiver. 'Get out,' she said shakily, but as he complied, and the door closed on his tall, white-coated figure, it brought her nothing but a disturbing feeling of emptiness.

Randall resisted the urge to slam the door hard enough to shatter it to pieces and walked briskly away from her room, towards one of his six surgical wards.

God, how he wanted her! *Still* she possessed that ability to send all reason flying from his mind, to be replaced by an all-encompassing urge to make love to her.

It took an effort to smile at the nurse who greeted him so enthusiastically when he arrived on Cedar ward.

'Hello!' she said, unable to conceal her pleasure.

'*You're* early tonight—you usually do your late-night round when I've gone to first break!'

Briefly, Randall tried and failed to imagine Kelly responding to him with such delight. 'I just wanted to see how the patient I operated on earlier is doing.'

'The emergency perforated duodenal ulcer?' queried the nurse.

'The very same.'

The nurse looked down at her Kardex. 'Mr Mulligan. He's making a good, uneventful recovery. He's fully conscious and his observations are stable. Would you like to see him?'

'Please.'

Mr Mulligan looked pale, but cheerful. 'Evening, Doctor,' he said hoarsely, as the nurse drew the curtains around the bed.

Randall smiled. 'Hello. How are you feeling?'

'My throat's a bit sore.'

'Nothing else?'

Mr Mulligan pointed to his abdomen. 'And here— just a bit.'

The nurse pulled back the sheet and Randall bent over to examine the wound. 'That looks fine,' he said, straightening up. 'Your sore throat is probably due to the anaesthetic—it's only temporary. And I'll be back tomorrow to deliver my usual stern lecture about the adverse effects of smoking, drinking and a poor diet!'

Mr Mulligan shrugged philosophically. 'Anything you say, Doc—just so long as I don't have to go through all this again!'

'Now that's gratitude for you!' joked Randall as

he stood aside to let the nurse pass, wondering why it should irritate him when she laughed far more loudly than his feeble joke merited.

He meticulously went to see every patient on his firm, then visited the intensive care unit to assess the man with the aortic aneurysm he'd operated on earlier that day. He had sewn a patch graft in place, but the man was by no means out of the wood yet.

Randall looked down at the white figure hooked up to the confusion of lines and tubes, than glanced at the nurse. 'How is he doing?'

Her face gave nothing away. 'He's stable. Just.'

But she spoke too soon. The aneurysm ruptured while they stood there, and although a highly qualified team of them battled to save the patient, it was to no avail.

It was very, very late when Randall went back to his room in the mess.

And in the quiet and stillness of the night, he could not get Kelly out of his mind, or the ache for her out of his body, and the long, cool shower he took before eventually turning in did little to dampen down the heat in his blood.

CHAPTER FOUR

AFTER a night spent chiefly drinking cups of coffee and staring sightlessly down at a textbook, Kelly crawled in to work the following morning feeling like something the cat had dragged in. She rarely made her face up for work; this morning it had been an absolute necessity to try to cover up the almost translucent pallor of her cheeks, and to attempt to conceal the dark shadows which were smudged beneath her eyes.

She thought she might have overdone it a bit when she saw Piers Redding, the casualty officer she was taking over from, give a double-take and make an appreciative little whistle beneath his breath.

'Wow!' he exclaimed. 'You look amazing!'

At least fifty of St Christopher's nurses would have adored such a compliment from Piers Redding—not so Kelly. 'Well, I feel like death,' she answered wryly. 'I didn't sleep a wink last night.'

Piers grinned. 'Which begs the usual question, but, being the gentleman I am, I'll refrain from asking it!'

Kelly's cheeks coloured. The cause of her sleepless night could so easily have been what Piers was teasing her about. Oh, lord. How she wished Randall Seton a hundred miles away from her! She picked up the two casualty cards which were lying on the doctor's desk. 'Who have we got?' she asked.

They bent over the desk together, their heads very close—she could even smell Piers' aftershave.

'Cubicle one's a fractured tib and fib waiting to go up to the orthopaedic ward. Cubicle two is a woman with query obstruction. I've bleeped the surgical registrar, and he's on his way down. Oh-oh, speak of the devil!' He looked up. 'Hi, Randall—there you are!'

Kelly stared at him.

He was wearing his theatre greens beneath his white coat, there was the dark shadow which covered that fabulously strong chin to show that he had not had time to shave, and he too didn't look as though he had got very much sleep the night before. 'Thanks,' he said briefly, and held his hand out towards Kelly, his eyes cold, his mouth hard.

She blinked at him, shocked by his weary appearance, even more shocked by the blatant hostility which was emanating from that lean, muscular frame. They had parted on bad terms last night, yes, but she had somehow expected that, during work hours at least, Randall of all people would have behaved in a civilised manner towards her. It seemed not.

'The casualty card, please, Doctor!' Randall bit out tersely, finding the way that she stood so close to the other casualty office almost unbearable.

Kelly handed him the card.

'And can I have a nurse to chaperon me?' he asked.

Kelly was finding it very difficult to think what she was supposed to be doing. 'I've—only just come on duty,' she told him, finding herself caught up in the cold gleam from the grey eyes.

'How absolutely *scintillating*,' he answered sarcastically. 'And now perhaps you'd see about finding me a nurse?'

Kelly glared at him.

'Don't worry, Mr Seton,' cooed a voice of treacle from behind him, and Staff Nurse Higgs, her blonde cap of hair gleaming like a halo, smiled up at him. 'Here I am!'

'Thanks, Nurse——' he glanced at her name-badge '—Higgs.'

'Call me Marianne,' answered the statuesque blonde immediately.

He smiled, and Kelly felt a murderous rage envelop her.

'Marianne,' he agreed easily. 'Come on then.'

Kelly watched them go, hating the way that Nurse Higgs was simpering up at him, and hating herself even more for feeling that way. She sighed as she picked up the phone and dealt with one of the local GPs who wanted to send a child with a query appendicitis into Casualty. Kelly wrote down the details and replaced the receiver.

Avoiding Randall wasn't just going to be difficult, she recognised, it was going to prove downright *impossible*. As the surgical registrar, he would need to be called down to Casualty every time a surgical emergency came through those doors, and every time that *she* was on duty as casualty officer, she was going to have to be the one to call him.

Hell!

What a nasty little trick fate had played in bringing Randall Seton back into her life, she thought, as the emergency telephone began to ring and she grabbed at the receiver.

The morning was so hectic that she didn't get a chance to think about anything, other than how to try to save the life of a twenty-eight-year-old man who had shot some very impure heroin into his body.

They battled for almost an hour, and when Kelly transferred him up to Intensive Care he was hanging on to life by a thread, his kidneys badly damaged.

There followed a stream of admissions, some to medical and some to surgical wards, and a small queue of surgical admissions built up since Randall was busy in Theatre, operating. Consequently, every time that Kelly walked near to the waiting area she was accosted by irate people, wanting to know why their relatives had not been seen.

'I'm very sorry,' said Kelly patiently, thinking that if she could have a penny for each time she had had to repeat this phrase she would be as rich as Croesus! 'But the surgeon who needs to see them before thay can be admitted is operating at the moment.'

'Then why can't we see another doctor?' demanded one woman, rather forcefully.

Kelly sighed. Now was not the time to start a discussion on hospital economics or government policy; patients, in her experience, did not like to be told that there simply were not enough doctors. 'Because I'm afraid that there isn't anyone else available,' she told them, with a bright smile which was supposed to allay their fears. She could see the receptionist waving a fistful of cards at her. 'Now, if you'll please excuse me, I must get on.'

On very little sleep, Kelly was thoroughly exhausted by the end of her shift, and there was barely time to do more that eat half of the salad sandwich for lunch which one of the student nurses had fetched for her. No wonder she'd lost weight since starting this job.

The consultant in charge of Casualty had devised a series of twelve-hour shifts for each of the three casualty officers, with an overlap on Friday and Saturday nights when the department was usually full to bursting.

At ten to six everything was quiet, and Kelly glanced at her watch. Ten minutes to go before Harry Wells was due to relieve her, and, knowing Harry, he was more likely to be ten minutes late than ten minutes early!

She stifled a yawn. Maybe she would be able to grab an hour's sleep before getting ready to go out. Warren wasn't collecting her until eight o'clock.

She had been dating the hospital administrator of St Christopher's for almost two months, though they rarely saw each other more than once or twice a week. He was intelligent, good-looking, and good company in a lot of ways. A bluntly spoken northerner, he seemed to approve of the fact that so far she had refused to let him do more than give her a brief goodnight kiss, saying, smilingly, that the best things in life were worth waiting for, and that he would 'give her time'. Secretly, she wondered if that time would ever come. Warren's kisses were pleasant, yes, she enjoyed them very much—but there was no way that they turned her into the wild wanton that Randall's kisses did. Perhaps that was a good thing, really. She wasn't sure that she liked the person she became in Randall's arms.

She certainly didn't respect her.

At precisely two minutes to six, and with no sign of her relief arriving, the red telephone began its shrilly insistent pealing, and with a resigned grimace Kelly lifted up the receiver, her face growing pale with shock when she heard the ambulance driver's terse statement.

'Gunshot wound to abdomen. Youth of seventeen. Condition critical. ETA three minutes.'

She got one of the nurses to put out an emergency bleep for Randall and for the crash team, then, running into the resuscitation-room, she pressed the emergency buzzer. Three nurses came running.

'Can you set up the resuscitation-room?' asked Kelly breathlessly. 'And get on to the blood bank— we've a gunshot wound on its way. I'm going out to the double doors to wait.'

She didn't have to wait long. The white-faced boy lying critically injured on the trolley looked so young. So very young. Kelly shuddered as she pulled the sheet back to see a gaping hole in his lower abdomen which had left some of his internal organs showing. They pushed the trolley straight into the emergency room, and to her relief she saw Randall waiting. But no crash team.

They lifted the boy over to to the trolley. 'I've bleeped the crash team,' said Kelly.

'They're answering another call,' said Randall frowning, his long fingers expertly assessing the extent of the injuries. 'Let's get some saline up.'

'What are his observations doing?' asked Kelly.

'BP eighty over thirty and falling,' answered the nurse, obviously frightened. 'Pulse a hundred and forty. And rising.'

He was in deep, deep shock. Kelly glued the pads of the heart monitor to the boy's chest, her heart sinking as she looked up at the screen to see the bright green but erratic tracing.

'He's going,' said Randall, and at the same time as he said it the monitor gave its high, monotonous shrilling which meant that the heart had stopped beating. Randall swiftly and sharply brought down the flat of his hand on to the boy's chest, while Kelly began to breathe into the mouthpiece, but they conducted the task knowing that it was doomed to failure; the boy was losing far more blood that they could possibly pump back in, and Kelly could see that the extent of his injuries was far worse that she had first thought.

'Let's get some more fluid in!' ordered Randall urgently.

But when the straight line, with its depressing long bleep, had been showing for five minutes, Randall straightened up and shook his head. 'That's it. I'm afraid we've lost him,' he said, his deep voice sombre, obviously as deeply affected as they all were. 'I'm very sorry, everyone.' And he peeled off his gloves and dropped them into the bin.

'Relatives?' Kelly asked the nurse shakily, when her boss, Mr Chalmers, the casualty consultant, came in, closely followed by the crash team, who took one look at all the debris of half opened packages which surrounded the dead body on the trolley, then turned and silently filed out again.

'I'll see the relatives, Kelly,' he told her. 'The police will want to speak to you and Randall. Are you OK?'

She nodded, glad that she had a boss sensitive enough to know how much death could still hurt, no matter how many times you saw it. She found Randall staring at her, the grey eyes soft with comprehension, and she swallowed the lump which rose in her throat.

'Where the hell *is* Harry Wells?' demanded Mr Chalmers.

'He *has* just had a new baby, sir,' said Kelly quickly.

'You mean his wife has just had a baby,' corrected Mr Chalmers drily. 'Harry's a damned sight too fond of the squash court. Oh, there you are, Wells.' He gave the gangling casualty office a disapproving stare. 'There's an RTA coming in in ten minutes— and make sure you're on time tomorrow night. Dr Hartley's had a rough enough day without you adding to her stress levels.' He turned to Kelly and Randall. 'The police are waiting for you in my office.'

Kelly nodded and walked over the sink to wash her hands, Randall joining her. How intimate it seemed to be sharing the same washbasin, thought Kelly suddenly, as he dolloped some antiseptic solution on to the palm of her hand without being asked.

He was frowning as he looked down at her. 'Are you sure you're OK?'

She nodded. 'It was pretty awful, wasn't it?'

'Yeah.' There was a pause. 'You never really get over the shock of seeing something like that.'

'Not even you?' she asked quietly.

He shook his head, a wry expression on his face. 'No, not even me. It's no different for men, Kelly. We hurt just the same, and nothing can make you immune to it, nothing. You don't suddenly find that you wake up one day and it doesn't affect you any more. And if you do, then you're in the wrong job.'

'And there was nothing we could have done?' She knew that, he knew that—but always there was the need for reinforcement, the need to dispel the quite unnecessary guilt you always felt when a life, and particularly a young life, just slipped away.

He shook his head. 'Nothing.' His grey gaze flickered over her. 'Do you get a lot of gunshot wounds around here?'

'That's the first I've ever seen. There are plenty of stabbings, though, and a fair bit of mugging. It's one of the reasons why I chose to live in the mess. I didn't really fancy walking home at all hours.'

'No,' he said thoughtfully. 'I don't blame you. Come on, we'd better go and give our statements.'

The statement-giving was mercifully brief, and

they both emerged from the office wearily. 'I'll walk your way,' said Randall. 'Unless you've any objections to that, of course,' he added sardonically.

Disappointedly, she simply shook her head. When he had been interacting with her as a fellow professional, everything had been fine. Now, it seemed, he was back to responding to her as a woman. She was too tired to retaliate, but curious anyway.

'I don't want to take you out of your way.'

'You won't be,' he said abruptly.

Kelly's eyebrows rose. 'But surely you're not living in the mess as well?'

'Why not?' His mouth was twisted into a cynical half-smile. 'You do.'

'But you're. . .' She hesitated, as their steps fell in line.

'I'm what, Kelly?' he enquired softly. 'Where did you imagine I'd be living? In some bloody great mansion up in Knightsbridge? It's all that excess baggage again, remember?'

The excess baggage which went with his title. Yes, she remembered. She gave him a rueful look as they reached her door. 'Sorry.'

'Mmm,' he said absently, but he was staring down into her face as though he had not heard her.

The grey glitter of his eyes drew her gaze inexorably towards his, as lost as some poor sailor lured by a siren on to the rocks. She did not know for how long they stood there, but somewhere she heard a clock strike the half-hour. Bang goes my sleep, thought Kelly dazedly, as she realised that she was staring up into Randall's face, and that there was a curious half-smile on his mouth, a strange gleam in his eyes.

'You look absolutely exhausted,' he observed.

'So do you,' she said, aware that a strand of hair had fallen out of the tight chignon. She brushed it behind her ear.

'And tense,' he added. 'Am I the cause of that tension, Kelly?'

Kelly shook her head. 'Not at the moment. It's been an exceptionally busy day, and I found all that, just now, in there——' she jerked her head in the direction from which they had just walked '—it was. . .horrible,' she finished starkly.

He raked a hand through his thick, dark hair. 'I know. And part of the trouble with this infernal job is that we take so much on board, and we never let it out, and somehow we're expected to cope with it.'

Her wide mouth quirked into a smile. 'You think that there should be counselling for doctors dealing with trauma?'

'Don't you?' he countered.

'Resources, resources, Doctor!' she chided, and realised that she was grinning, and that he was grinning too, and that his eyes had darkened, and— oh, lord—how could a smile set your senses singing, start a weary body zinging? And Randall had gone very still, very tense. Had her body somehow communicated its fascination for him?

'God, I want to make love to you,' he said suddenly.

Kelly's lids dropped down to shield the disappointment in her eyes. Of course he did. She opened her eyes and gave him a chilly smile. 'Should I be flattered by such a remarkably direct statement, Randall? Because I'm not. And I really don't think that my boyfriend would like to hear you saying things like that.'

He stiffened and his eyes narrowed. 'Your *boyfriend*?'

She felt an intense kind of rage at his incredulous tone. Just what did he imagine? That she was incapable of sustaining an adult relationship? Or that she had been pining away for *him* for all these years? She gave a brittle little laugh. 'I'm sorry you seem to find that peculiar——'

'Who is he?' he demanded, and his voice sounded so odd and so savage that Kelly involuntarily took a step back.

'Who *is* he?' he repeated.

She saw no reason not to tell him. If he realised that Warren worked in the same hospital, then it might make him leave her alone. 'Warren Booth,' she told him. 'The——'

'Hospital administrator,' he finished grimly.

'You know him?'

'I've met him,' he said, still in that same grim tone. 'You surprise me, Kelly.'

'Oh? And why's that?' she queried coolly.

The grey eyes became shuttered. 'I value my career far too much to give you an honest answer to that particular question. Let's just say that he isn't my kind of person,' he answered tersely.

'I can imagine,' said Kelly, with an acid smile.

He glowered at her. 'But I find it rather difficult to trust anyone who happens to be in management.'

'And it's that kind of attitude,' she bit out, realising as she said it that she was doing nothing more than echoing Warren's very own words to her, 'which creates divisions between management and staff!'

'The divisions exist,' he told her quietly, 'because they have conflicting interests. All the management are interested in is saving money by cutting staff.'

'How simplistic!' she mocked. 'While all doctors are interested in is saving lives, I suppose?'

'Actually, yes,' he answered, very quietly, and his grey eyes glittered. 'At least, I am. Aren't you?'

With that clever sharp tongue, he had made it sound as though she was saying something very different from her intended defence of Warren. And why was she bothering to defend Warren to Randall anyway?

'Oh, that isn't what I meant at all and you know it, *damn* you, Randall Seton!' she snapped. 'I hate you!' she finished, and made as if to move away from him. But though her words sounded authentic, her heart knew the truth as she stared into that heart-stoppingly handsome face.

His mouth twisted in the parody of a smile as he caught her by the waist, imprisoning her there, though less by the force of his hands than by the enchanting silver dazzle of his eyes. He stared down at her for a long moment before he dropped on to her soft mouth a cold, cynical kiss which, though brief, none the less left her trembling helplessly in his arms before he let her go, his hands falling to his sides, his fists clenched white, as though he were going to punch somebody.

'You may hate me,' he ground out, 'but you still want me, don't you, just as much as I still want you? And I'm giving you fair warning that I intend to have you, Kelly.'

And he turned and walked off, leaving Kelly staring blankly after him, shaking with some unnamed emotion, her fingertips touching her mouth, as if by doing that she could preserve the brief memory of his lips on hers forever.

CHAPTER FOUR

WITH her heart hammering like crazy, Kelly closed the door behind Randall, trying to rid herself of the yearning which his kiss had produced.

She began to undress, her hands still shaking as she wrapped herself in a towelling bathrobe and went down the chilly corridor to shower. She was back in her room drying her hair when the telephone rang.

It was Warren, saying that he was running half an hour late. 'Pressure of work,' he complained.

'It doesn't matter,' said Kelly, wishing that she felt a bit more enthusiastic about going out.

'Can you dress up a bit, darling?' he asked her.

Kelly's heart sank. That didn't sound very much like the quiet dinner for two she had been hoping he would suggest. 'Why? Are we going somewhere special?'

'Fairly. One of the consultants is having a drinks party. He's invited me—and a guest, of course.'

'Which consultant?'

'Dr Berry—the physician.'

'Tonight?'

'Yes.'

'That's a little short notice, surely?' asked Kelly rather crossly, knowing that Warren would have walked to the end of the planet for something like a consultant's party. 'Were they short on numbers or something?'

'It's an honour to be asked,' said Warren firmly, an unmistakable note of disapproval in his voice. 'It's usually only the clinical staff who get invited to these affairs. So run along, darling, and I'll see you in half an hour.'

Kelly found herself irritated with his remark. For goodness' sake! She seemed to be irritated with everything today, and she knew who had instigated her niggly mood.

Half an hour later she opened the door to Warren's ring on the bell, to see him blink at her slightly disconcertedly. He was dressed, as usual, in a conservative grey suit with a white shirt, and a dark blue tie bearing the hospital crest. Kelly hated that tie; she had bought him a wildly coloured silk one for his birthday, but so far he hadn't worn it.

'Good heavens!' he exclaimed, as his eyes skimmed quickly over her slender form.

She gave a twirl. 'Don't you like it?' He had never seen the outfit before. She was dressed in an exquisitely cut dress of tawny silk which brought out the auburn lights of her hair, which she had left loose to ripple all the way down her back. Her high-heeled black shoes made her slim legs seem endless, and she had deliberately worn seamed silk stockings instead of her usual tights, wanting the feel of some soft, sensual material on her thighs for a change. She had not stopped to ask herself why.

Warren gulped. 'It's—er—er. . .' He cleared his throat. 'Do you think it's really *suitable*, Kelly?'

Kelly knew that she was not in a good mood, and the sight of Warren tugging anxiously on his earlobe was not doing anything to improve it. 'What's wrong with it?' she demanded, and he raised his fair eyebrows when he heard her mulish tone. 'Don't you like the dress?'

'It isn't the *dress*. It's. . .'

'What then?'

'Your hair.'

'My *hair*?' she asked in disbelief. She had just washed it and spent an age drying it. 'What's the matter with my hair?'

'You usually wear it up.'

A forbidden, tantalising memory of Randall loosening the pins to set it free invaded her mind with persistent and exacting detail, and she tried desperately to brush it aside.

She stared at Warren—so tall, so fair, so smart and reliable in his grey suit—and willed the feeling of rebellion to go away.

It didn't.

Kelly sighed. 'I know I usually wear it up,' she said. 'And I fancy wearing it down for a change. OK?'

She smiled, and at the sight of her smile he relaxed. Kelly saw the little glint in his pale blue eyes.

'Actually,' he said, and his voice held a new, possessive note, 'I prefer it up. Am I allowed to have a preference?'

This was getting out of hand, Kelly decided. 'Of

course you are,' she said crisply. 'But tonight it's staying like this.'

'I see.' Warren hesitated. 'It just doesn't look so. . .'

Kelly waited. 'So what?'

'Neat.'

The vision suddenly horrified her. Was that what she had become? A neat, tidy person, with her neat, tidy boyfriend? She put her chin firmly in the air, and the thick, chestnut waves rippled in Pre-Raphaelite disarray. 'I'll tell you what, Warren,' she said, her green eyes sparking with unaccustomed fire, 'I'm really not in the mood to be told how I can or how I can't wear my hair, and I've had a bitch of a day, to be perfectly frank. So why don't you go to the party on your own? OK?'

A frown appeared, just visible beneath Warren's blond fringe. 'What's got into you all of a sudden?'

Randall has, thought Kelly. And shuddered. 'Nothing. I'm sorry. I'm tired. You go.'

He shook his head with that calm yet emphatic air he had perfected, the one she used to find comforting, safe, reassuring, but tonight she found irritating. 'And miss being seen with the best-looking woman in the hospital on my arm? No way!'

Too tired to argue, and since she hadn't eaten a thing and there was no food in the fridge, Kelly let him lead her down to his brand-new family saloon.

She sat in the passenger seat, clasped her hands in her lap and tried to smile, and Warren leaned over and lingeringly kissed her passive lips.

'Maybe we should see about giving you my famous

cure for tiredness,' he whispered meaningfully. 'It's never failed me yet.'

Kelly swallowed, realising that just the thought of it left her completely cold. 'Warren, I——'

'We'll discuss it later,' he promised, in a husky whisper.

Kelly stared sightlessly out of the window, feeling as though all her chickens were coming home to roost. Was Warren planning a big seduction tonight? And if he was, then it couldn't be more ill-timed if he had tried. She tried to relax as he put on some soft music while the car gathered speed, but it was difficult.

Dr Berry lived in a predictably large and comfortable house some distance from the hospital. In the driveway were other newish, and rather more opulent, cars. Inside, they were greeted by the eminent physician, and his well-preserved wife, who looked Kelly up and down with sharp eyes.

'Nice to see you both!' said Dr Berry. 'Come and get a drink! Warren—I've just the person I want you to meet.' He waved his hand in the direction of the chairman of the hospital trust, and Warren drew in a breath of excitement. 'Do you know Charles?'

Warren almost drooled at the sound of the physician using the chairman's Christian name. 'I've met him, of course, but——'

'Come and talk to him.' And Dr Berry led Warren away.

'There are drinks inside,' said Mrs Berry, but her eyes were elsewhere, distractedly scanning the room for more important fish to fry than a mere casualty officer.

'Thanks,' said Kelly, feeling somewhat redundant as she took a glass of white wine from one of the waitresses who were circulating the room with trays of drinks. She stood sipping it, until a haematologist she knew only very vaguely came over to chat to her. He was pleasant, if not the most exciting company in the world, and he obviously found Kelly very attractive. He started telling her about an article on platelets he'd just had accepted by the *British Medical Journal*, and Kelly found herself drifting off into a little world of her own.

'So would you like to?' he was saying.

Kelly blinked. 'Sorry?'

'Have dinner with me one night?'

But she scarcely heard him; the room swayed, tipped off balance as Randall walked in.

And though it was crowded, his grey eyes found her immediately, as if compelled to do so, and her heart began to beat painfully hard in her chest as his gaze deliberately swept over every inch of her.

It was a candid, sexual appraisal, and he took his time, his mouth softening into the sweetest caress of a smile as his eyes lingered on the swell of her breasts the longest. Unlike Warren, Randall obviously found the sight of her very pleasing indeed.

She had to get out of here.

'Please excuse me,' she managed to croak to the haematologist, and pushed her way through the small groups of people, away from Randall and that dangerous stare of his.

But she went with the resignation of someone walking the plank, knowing that it was inevitable he would follow her.

The plants in the garden were a mystery to her, but she pretended to look, even while every sense she possessed waited. Anticipated. She bristled as she heard the soft tread behind her, and she closed her eyes, afraid that he would read in them the glittering need to feast her gaze on him too.

'You can open your eyes now, Kelly,' came an amused, dry voice. 'And stop trembling like a Victorian heroine. I'm not planning to eat you.'

She kept her eyes shut. 'Go away.'

'Why?'

She opened them then. Why did he have to be so attractive? 'What is it with you?' she demanded. 'Why won't you leave me alone?'

He raised his eyebrows. 'Stop over-reacting. Let's go for a walk.'

'So you can try to seduce me?'

He smiled. 'If you like. But I was rather hoping we might talk. We used to talk a lot, you and I.'

'It's a pity we didn't stick to talking,' she said, on a bitter note.

'Come on. Let's look at all these plants.'

'I don't know anything about plants.'

'I know that,' he said patiently.

'How?'

'I remember you telling me, city-girl.' He saw her

look of disbelief. 'Don't look so surprised. I remember everything about you, Kelly. Truly.'

She shook her head, trying not to warm to his charm. 'I'm here with someone.'

The curve of his smile became a derisive line. 'I know. With Warren, who is at present almost genuflecting in front of Sir Charles Ledbury.' He held a bottle of champagne aloft. 'Come on. Let's go and share this. We're both off duty.'

'How did you get hold of that?' she asked curiously.

'I batted my eyelashes at one of the waitresses,' he told her shamelessly. 'Look, there's a table down there, beneath the stars. Come and drink this champagne, and I give you my word that I will behave with the utmost decorum.' He gave a mock bow— superbly executed, thought Kelly reluctantly—and some glimmer of amusement which lurked deep in the grey eyes made her unable to repress a giggle in response.

He stared down at her for a long moment. 'Thank God,' he told her on a sigh. 'I actually thought that I'd lost my ability to make you laugh.'

Vexed and flattered by him, seduced by the potency of his charm, and the scent of the tobacco plants and the warm, seductive embrace of the sultry evening air, Kelly found herself following him down to the bottom of the garden, to where a white, wrought-iron table gleamed out at them from the dusk.

He pulled her chair back for her and she sat down, accepting the glass of champagne he handed to her.

'So, what are you doing here?' she asked coolly.

'The same thing as you, I should imagine. Perhaps not. You're here accompanying Warren, who sees the object of this party as some kind of PR exercise. Am I right?'

Damn him and his perspicacity! 'These affairs which involve work are never entirely social,' she countered. 'Don't tell me you're here with the sole intention of having a good time?'

'Not at all. I came here with the sole intention of finding you.'

Her hand threatened to tremble; she took another sip of the cold, fizzy wine, and it flooded her stomach with a welcome warmth. 'Oh? Should I be flattered?'

'I wouldn't have thought so,' he said wryly.

'What do you want to talk to me about?'

'Your career.'

Kelly was astounded. Admit it, she thought—she was expecting—hoping for?—yet another proposition. Work had been the last thing on her mind.

'Why my career?'

'I'm interested.'

'What exactly do you want to know?' she asked curiously.

He sipped his champagne, his grey eyes studying her over the rim of his glass. 'Fill me in. I assume you're doing the casualty job as part of your surgical experience?'

She had said the words so many times, to her tutors, her peers, her parents, yet still it hurt to have to say them again. She carefully schooled her face into the nonchalant expression she had chosen to accompany these particular words. 'No. I'm not going to be a surgeon.'

Randall was about to take another sip of his wine, but seemed to change his mind, and he put the crystal glass abruptly down on the table. '*What*?'

'I don't want. . .' But that was just too big a betrayal ever to pass her lips. 'I'm not going to be a surgeon,' she said firmly. 'I'm going to be a general practitioner instead.'

He frowned. 'I don't believe it.'

'It's true,' she said quietly.

'But that was your thing! That was your ambition. God, you were so passionate about it—you slayed me with your passion.'

She saw the look of disbelieving censure on his face, and now she felt like Judas. 'I was seventeen at the time, Randall,' she reminded him. 'A lot of people back-track on their youthful dreams.'

'Not you.' He stared at her thoughtfully. 'You won the St Christopher's gold medal in surgery; got a distinction in your finals too. Didn't you?'

Kelly's heart pounded. 'How on earth do you know that?'

'Oh, come on, Kelly, the results are published in some of the medical journals.'

'You looked my results up?'

'Sure.'

'Why?' It came out breathlessly.

'I was interested.'

Some eager little hope fizzled out, like a spent match. All those years, all those nine long years, he had known where she had been studying. And not once had he bothered to come and see her. She wanted to throw her glass of champagne in his face and run back inside, demand that Warren take her home. But she knew that her legs would not carry her, and that Warren would be merely peeved if she interrupted his talk with the precious Sir Charles. Instead, she managed an empty, almost bored smile. 'So now you know.'

He shook his head. 'No, I don't. Just tell me why, Kelly? Why did you welsh out on your ambition?'

Frustrated, bitter and angry, she turned on him, slamming her glass down to join his. 'OK, I'll tell you why. Because I'm a woman—it's as simple as that!'

His eyes narrowed. 'And what's that supposed to mean?'

She glowered. 'Don't be so obtuse! It means exactly what it says! Think about it. Surgery is a powerful speciality, and it's run by very powerful men. Because that's what it is, essentially—a men's club. Jobs for the boys. Women aren't welcome, in exactly the same way that lots of golf clubs have rooms which won't admit women. But in surgery it's much more insidious than that. There are laws which say that women mustn't be discriminated against——'

'And you're saying that you've been discriminated against?'

'It's more subtle than out-and-out discrimination. It's having to prove yourself, not twice as good as the next man, but ten times as good! And even then, it's still not good enough! After a while, that kind of attitude wears you down. And if you don't believe

me, then look around. Look at the drop-out rate of
women in surgery. And the further up the ladder,
the harder it gets, especially if you've got family
commitments. How many women consultants of
surgery do *you* know, Randall, hmm?'

He said nothing for a moment, just continued to
look at her with that dark, unreadable expression on
his face, but Kelly felt confident that he, of all
people, would understand. He had hurt her badly
when she was young, yes, but professionally he had
been her champion. Randall would understand.

His mouth curved disdainfully. 'You disappoint
me, Kelly. I thought you had more guts than just to
throw it in at the first hurdle.'

The disapproval which glittered from the angry
grey eyes was almost unbearable. 'What do you
know about it?' she demanded. 'You're a——'

But he cut across her ruthlessly. 'Don't bore me
with all that "you're a man" stuff! We're not talking
about me, are we? We're talking about *you*! Yes,
you're a woman—an intelligent and gifted woman!
A woman who defied all the odds to get to medical
school in the first place! A woman who drew the
recognition of the medical establishment to win half
the prizes of her year!' He was on his feet now, had
moved to stand in front of her, towering over her,
his face dark with rage. 'A woman with no family
commitments in her way, who could get right to the
top of the bloody tree—*effortlessly*! And what does
she do? She convinces herself that she's a victim,
and she damn well gives it up!'

Kelly was on her own feet now, his words stinging

her so bitterly because she recognised the truth in them. 'Have you quite finished?' she demanded, white-faced.

'No, I have not finished! I haven't even started!' And he hauled her into his arms to crush his mouth down on to hers.

She felt the anger flooding hotly from him to her; her own anger pulsed through her veins with its fiery heat, but within seconds there was no longer anger but a crazy, aching need to make love which had smouldered for nine long years and never gone away.

'Randall,' she whispered helplessly against his lips as he moved his hand to cup her breast with such fervour that the nipple peaked into immediate life against his palm through the thin silk of her dress. She felt her knees weaken, felt the hot, heavy rush of desire, as thick as honey, as intoxicating as strong liquor.

'Randall,' she whispered again, making no move to stop him as he pushed her behind the concealing wall of a rhododendron bush, covering her mouth all the time with that sweet, penetrating kiss. 'We shouldn't,' she managed, on a breathless note of wonder, coiling her long fingers into the thick black hair, her actions making mockery of her words.

'Oh, yes, we should,' he said huskily. 'Darling, we must, you know we must. . .'

He was pulling up the flimsy silk of her dress, sliding his hand all the way up over her silk-clad leg, until he found the bare thigh which lay above the lacy rim of her stocking-top, and he made a murmured sound which was midway between a groan of pleasure, and a protest. 'Dear God!' he exclaimed. 'Why the hell did you wear stockings?'

Through the hazy whirlpool of desire, Kelly whispered foggily, 'Don't you like them?'

'Kelly, Kelly, Kelly. . .' His voice was frantic, urgent. 'Every fantasy I've concocted about you over the last nine years features you wearing stockings, me peeling them off. Dear God, I want to lay you down on the grass and make love to you right now, right here,' he said on a note of frustrated despair.

Kelly never knew what might have happened next had she not heard her name being called. She didn't ever dare to try to imagine, because the ignominy of being discovered making love in the grounds of Dr Berry's house was too much to contemplate.

'Kelly!'

With a stifled profanity, Randall immediately smoothed down her skirt, raked his hand through the thick, dark waves of his hair, moved away from her, picked up his glass of champagne, and downed it in one.

'Kelly!'

It was Warren. Her face burning with shame, Kelly quickly emerged from behind the bush to see Warren walking down the garden towards them, his head darting from side to side as he searched her out.

'Leave this to me,' said Randall curtly.

'*No*!' she turned on him angrily. 'You've done enough for one evening——'

'Have I?' he mocked, and her colour heightened further.

'I'll deal with it,' she said coldly. 'So go.'

But he didn't go. He just stood there quite calmly as Warren approached them.

'There you are, Kelly.' Warren's shoulders stiffened. 'Oh, good evening, Lord Rousay.'

Please, Warren, don't kow-tow to him, prayed Kelly silently, despising herself for what she had almost allowed to happen.

'I'd rather not use my title for work, if you don't mind,' said Randall curtly. 'And I'd like a word with you, please. In private.'

'Randall, *no!*' beseeched Kelly. 'I'll deal with it.'

Warren looked from Kelly to Randall, suspicion finally dawning in his eyes. Something ugly entered his face. 'I've got a pretty good idea what it is that you want to say,' he sneered. 'And I would have thought that you'd be able to find your own woman, without encroaching on someone else's property. Come, Kelly. We're going.'

Randall frowned, his face hard. 'You don't describe this woman. . .*any* woman, for that matter—as your property,' he said in a harsh voice.

Kelly had also bristled at the implication that she was Warren's property, but her sole intention was to dissolve the whole ghastly affair without causing a scene. She gave Randall a beseeching look, then turned and preceded Warren, walking towards the house, her head held high in the air, not even glancing again in Randall's direction.

* * *

Warren didn't say a word all the way back to the hospital, and Kelly took one look at the forbidding set of his jaw, and kept her silence also.

He walked with her to her room, and she hesitated, utterly ashamed of herself. 'Would you like some coffee?' she asked tentatively.

'I could use a drink,' he said shortly.

She poured two whiskies, and he drained his in one, then turned to face her, his face white, an odd look in his blue eyes. 'Warren, I'm so sorry——'

'Don't bother to try to apologise or try to explain,' he cut in, and even his voice sounded unfamiliar. 'I'm not a fool. Either you were just kissing Seton or he's taken to wearing lipstick.'

Kelly's fingers fluttered up to cover her bare lips. 'Oh, God,' she whispered.

'Save your prayers!' he sneered, then helped himself to another whisky without asking, drained that too, and an ugly flush invaded his cheeks. 'What is it about him, huh? That you act like some kind of tramp in his arms?'

'I didn't——' she protested feebly.

'Really? That's why the two top buttons of your dress just happen to be undone, is it? Why him, Kelly—just tell me that? Is it the title? Is that what turns you on? Do you imagine for one moment that anything will come of it? If you're holding out hopes of becoming the next Lady Rousay, I wouldn't bank on it.'

'Warren,' she said quietly, 'please don't say any more.'

But he ignored her, ranting on like some fanatic

on a soap-box. 'We could have had it all, Kelly, you know we could! We're alike, you and me — the same kind of background, the same kind of struggles. We *understand* each other. It could have been us against the world.'

Kelly stared at him in bewilderment. 'But I never said——'

'Oh, no, you never said,' he interrupted bitterly. 'I thought I'd give you time to say it. I thought I'd wait, hold back, play the gentleman. Well, more fool me, when all the time you couldn't wait to drop your——'

Kelly whitened. 'That's enough, Warren! You've said enough!'

There was a high, disturbing pitch to his voice. 'I haven't said nearly enough! That's all he wants, you know. He's only after one thing, and once he's got it, he'll——'

'Get out,' she said, in a low, appalled voice. 'Get out, Warren, before you say anything else you might regret.'

But he didn't move, just looked at her, his eyes wild and unfamiliar, bright with whisky. 'Yes, maybe you're right, Kelly. Maybe the time for talking's over. Maybe I did a little too much talking, when all the time I should have just given you what you're obviously crying out for. . .'

And he lunged for her.

Caught by surprise, unbalanced by a strength emphasised by his determination, Kelly half fell on to the carpet, her eyes wide and frightened. 'No,' she whimpered, as she saw the expression in the pale eyes. 'Please, no. . .'

'Oh, *yes*,' he sneered, and he pushed her to the ground, falling on top of her, pushing all the breath out of her lungs as his mouth, reeking of whisky, began to cling slackly on to hers, his knee brutally pushing her thighs apart.

But the contact only lasted seconds, because the mouth was removed almost as soon as it had clamped itself on to hers, and Kelly turned her terrified gaze upwards to see that Randall had bodily picked Warren off her and was holding him by the shoulders, his face a study in naked rage. There was a stunned silence as Warren's eyes focused on the dark face above him. Don't hit him, thought Kelly, as she saw the grey eyes harden with contempt.

'I think the lady said *no*,' Randall said, in a voice tight with anger, showing the restraint he was obviously exercising over his temper.

And Kelly surprised a look of such malicious fury on Warren's face that she shuddered, and realised that by letting him off Randall had done the wrong thing entirely. For Warren came from a culture where men fought over women, where women were second-rate. If they had fought, they could have shaken hands, gone off and had a beer together.

'You'd better go, Warren,' she whispered.

'Yes, go,' said Randall tightly, 'before I tear you limb from limb. And if you ever come anywhere near her again I'll do it anyway. Do I make myself clear?'

There was a quiet, intimidating flavour of menace

in his last gritted sentence, and Kelly could see the fear in Warren's eyes.

'Do I?' he repeated ominously.

'Yes.' And fixing them both with a final baleful stare, Warren stumbled out of the room without another word.

After he'd gone, neither she nor Randall spoke for a minute. He was standing very still, with his fists clasped into whitened knuckles by his side, and she could see that he was having difficulty holding on to his temper.

'Are you OK?' he said, and his voice held a kind of tremor.

She gave him a blank, bitter kind of stare. 'What do you think? Yes, I'm OK. I don't know about Warren though.'

'Warren?' His brows flew up incredulously. 'For God's sake, Kelly. How the hell can you protect him, after what he tried to do to you?' he exploded.

'I'm not trying to protect him, I'm trying to understand him! And what do you think we tried to do to him?' she demanded, her voice wobbling as reaction set in. 'Humiliate him? Make him crawl?'

'Of course we didn't. What happened between us in the garden——'

'Forget it.'

He ignored her. 'Shouldn't have happened——'

'I said *forget* it!'

'No.' He came to within two feet of her. 'I'm not going to forget it. I can't. Can you?'

She turned away but he momentarily caught her

by the arm, and even that brief touch of his hand made her blood race with excitement.

'Listen to me, Kelly. I didn't plan what happened. I certainly didn't expect it to get so out of hand, so quickly. I'm sorry if Warren was hurt, but you know, and I know, that he was the wrong man for you. But even given that what we did was wrong, that does not excuse his behaviour here. What on earth do you think would have happened if I hadn't walked in when I did? He could have *raped* you, for God's sake!'

'If it's plaudits you're after, then jolly well done,' she said tiredly.

'What I want is for you to make a complaint against him. He should be reported to the police. And you know that.'

Just the thought of re-enacting what had happened before a third party filled Kelly with a nameless kind of dread. 'No!' She tossed her head vehemently and the waves shimmered in a copper haze. 'I want the matter dropped,' she said fiercely. 'Do you understand, Randall? Dropped and forgotten.'

His grey eyes were very serious. 'And what if he comes back?'

'I don't believe he will. And I have a lock on my door.'

He was standing only inches away, with the soft line of his sculpted mouth within kissing distance. She still wanted him. Would she never be free of the torment of wanting him? Sick at heart, she turned away, and this time he did not stop her. 'And now, if you've quite finished, I'd like to get to bed.'

'Darling——'

It was the final straw; soft words could tug with such power at her resolve. She turned on him, her eyes fierce, shaking inside at the almost tender way he used the endearment. '*No*, Randall! No! I don't want to hear what you've got to say! Every time you come into my life you turn it upside down and ruin it, one way or another, and I don't like it. Neither do I need it.'

There was a long silence, broken only by the sound of their breathing.

'Do I make my point?' she said, in an empty little voice.

He stared at her for a moment before he shrugged his broad, elegant shoulders in an gesture of acceptance, but his eyes were now cold and as hard as metal. She had never seen him look like that before, she realised, her heart inexplicably sinking.

'Crystal-clear,' he answered icily. He turned and walked out of the room, and Kelly turned the key in the door behind him, the tears beginning to slide down her cheeks at last.

CHAPTER FIVE

THE following morning the alarm-clock shrilled into harsh and unwelcome life at five a.m., and Kelly struggled to wake up.

Rubbing her eyes, she sat up in bed, her tousled hair falling all over her bare shoulders, her body cool and naked beneath the sheets, and she felt a slow heat rise in her face as she remembered Randall kissing her so passionately in the garden, and of her frightening response to his ardour. And the ghastly conclusion to the whole evening, with Warren leaping on her like a man possessed.

But it had happened; now it must be forgotten. She had decided to ignore what had happened, and she still had to work with both men. What it essentially boiled down to was that Warren had been both hurt and a little worse for wear, and that was why he had behaved so aggressively.

But she shuddered as she stood beneath the shower, and she tried not to think about what *could* have happened if Randall had not walked in when he had done.

She showered and dressed, then, putting her stethoscope and pager into the pocket of a clean white coat, she set off to the canteen for some breakfast.

The first person she saw was Randall. He was seated by one of the windows, scanning the pages of a textbook which was propped up against the salt and pepper pots, while he ate an enormous plateful of bacon and eggs. His hair was ruffled, and there were dark shadows beneath his eyes.

He glanced up at her, his eyes flicking briefly over her, and he gave her only the most cursory nod before turning back to his book.

Kelly turned away and moved like a robot over towards the counter, frozen by the indifference in that cold, grey stare, her hunger gone, but just to have walked out would have been a complete giveaway.

It hurt.

It hurt like hell.

But that had been what she had wanted, wasn't it? She had asked him to leave her alone, and now it seemed as though he was complying with her wishes. She found herself remembering his devastatingly critical words to her last night, when she'd told him that she did not intend pursuing surgery.

'Morning, ducks!' beamed the woman behind the counter. 'Cooked breakfast for you?'

Kelly shook her head. 'Just toast and coffee, thanks.'

The woman gave her a reproving stare as she put two pieces of toast, butter and marmalade on to a plate. 'You'll waste away, Doctor! There's nothing of you as it is!'

'I eat enough!' protested Kelly.

She carried her tray through the room, her head held high as she deliberately sat on the opposite side of the restaurant to Randall, but he didn't even look up from his book.

He left before she did, and she allowed herself to watch his retreating frame. Heavens, but he had the most amazing body she had ever seen. Tall and rangy and musuclar. And with the broadest shoulders.

Angry with her obsession with the man, she pushed the half eaten piece of toast away, and walked down to A & E.

She went straight in at the deep end, because, as Harry Wells was handing over to her, a middle-aged man was rushed in with chest pain. He was white and sweating and very anxious, and his wife was hysterical, which was only compounding his fears.

'He's not going to *die*, is he, Doctor?' the woman demanded frantically, grabbing hold of Kelly's arm.

Kelly gently but firmly disengaged her, and caught a student nurse's eye. 'We're doing everything we can for him,' she said gently. 'Nurse here will take you into the relatives' room and give you a cup of tea, and you can see him very shortly.'

Kelly went back into the cubicle and bent down to speak to the patient. 'Have you a lot of pain, Mr Dance?'

He nodded, his hand indicating the top part of his chest. 'Yes, Doctor,' he gasped. 'It's like a ton of bricks crashing down on my chest, and the pain goes down my arm too.'

Kelly quickly wrote up some intra-muscular morphine and some oral aspirin, and handed the drug chart to the nurse. 'Let's give him these as quickly as possible,' she said.

The drugs were administered, and as the nurse recorded Mr Dance's pulse, respiration and blood-pressure, Kelly started fixing the ECG electrodes to his chest.

This will help us to get a good look at your heart,' she told him, but the morphine was already taking effect and Mr Dance was in a hazy state of euphoria.

''S'nice,' he mumbled dreamily.

Kelly finished the ECG and bleeped the medical registrar, and was just studying the tracing when he arrived and glanced at the trace-out over her shoulder.

'Hi,' he said. 'How is he?'

'Calmer. I've given him a shot of morphine,' replied Kelly as she showed him the ECG. 'There's definite ST elevation on his electrocardiogram.'

He nodded. 'Mild infarction by the look of it. We'll get him up to CCU as soon as possible for observation. Though I'll have to transfer someone to the medical ward before I can arrange a bed. I'll do that now.' He picked up the receiver and dialled the coronary care number.

'Right,' said Kelly, and went to find a nurse to stay with Mr Dance until he could be admitted.

She was then called to see a middle-aged man who was complaining of a sore eye.

'Looks like a classic case of conjunctivitis to me,' confided the staff nurse.

Kelly picked up the casualty card and looked at it. 'We'll see,' she said.

The eye *did* have the familiar redness of conjunctivitis, Kelly decided, and she was unable to see any foreign body when she examined him with an ophthalmoscope. Nevertheless, she took a full history with her usual thoroughness.

'Have you suffered any injury to the eyes, Mr Marshall?' she asked.

He shook his head. 'No, Doctor.'

'Can I ask if you've been doing anything which might have inadvertently damaged your eye?'

'Can't think of anything.'

But Kelly had noticed a plaster on the man's finger. 'What have you done to your finger?'

'Oh, that's just a blister,' he replied. 'Been doing too much hammering.'

'Hammering?'

'Aye. Been putting an extension on to the back of the house for the missus.'

An idea had occurred to Kelly. 'I'm going to send you upstairs to have your eye X-rayed,' she told him.

Half an hour later he was back, and Kelly stood in the office with the eye surgeon, looking at the X-ray.

'You see——' he pointed at the film '—there's a sliver of metal at the back of the eye which must have shot in there while he was hammering. Easily missed. You did well, Kelly. We'll remove it later under general anaesthetic.'

And Kelly blushed with pride when the eye surgeon smiled at her and said very quietly, 'Well done, my dear, you've probably saved that man's eye.'

It was rare moments like that, she thought, which made being a doctor absolutely unbeatable.

The department was then relatively quiet for a couple of hours, and Kelly spent it usefully employed in reading the job advertisements in the *BMJ*. She was doing her own training scheme for general practice. She needed to do six months each in four different specialities before she could qualify as a GP. After A & E, she was required to do medicine, psychiatry and obstetrics and gynaecology. She *had* intended to do all her jobs at St Christopher's, the hospital where she had trained and been happy, but now she recognised that she would no longer be able to do that. Not if Randall was going to be working here for the next two years. . .

Her reverie was interrupted by Staff Nurse Higgs, who had just arrived on duty, her cold blue eyes narrowing as she saw Kelly. 'Oh, it's you!' she said ungraciously.

Resisting sarcasm, Kelly summoned up a smile. 'Good morning!'

Ignoring the pleasantry, Nurse Higgs fiddled with her fob watch. 'There's a patient in cubicle four.'

'With?'

Nurse Higgs dropped the casualty card on the desk in front of Kelly. 'Top of the finger chopped off. She brought it in wrapped up in a handkerchief. We've packed it in ice.'

'How's the bleeding?' asked Kelly crisply.

'We've stemmed it.'

'Good.'

Nurse Higgs gave a sly smile. 'Shall I bleep the surgeon for you?'

'I'll do it. But I'd better take a look at her first,' said Kelly firmly as she got to her feet.

Nurse Higgs raised her eyebrows. 'Of course, you *would* want to ring him yourself, I suppose.'

Kelly drew her eyebrows together at the tone in the nurse's voice. 'Sorry?'

'Mr Seton—the surgeon.'

'Yes, I know that Mr Seton is the surgeon,' answered Kelly impatiently. 'I just don't understand what point you're trying to make.'

Another sly smile as Nurse Higgs shrugged her shoulders. 'Just that you were seen at the party together last night.'

'Yes?'

'*Kissing*. Kissing Mr Seton, that is.'

Kelly flexed her fingers deep in the pockets of her white coat, and fixed the staff nurse with a steady stare, hoping that she wouldn't ruin everything by blushing like a schoolgirl. 'And since when has kissing been a crime?'

'Well, just that you arrived with Mr Booth——'

'Listen,' Kelly cut across the girl firmly. 'I'm here to do a job, Nurse Higgs, and so are you. That job happens to be the care of patients, not swapping idle hospital gossip. So if you'd like to come and help me in cubicle four, I can get on.'

'Certainly, *Doctor*,' answered Nurse Higgs mulishly.

It's nothing more than a personality clash, Kelly told herself, as she pulled back the curtains of cubicle four. It happens. But it was difficult to deal with the sort of insidious insubordination the staff nurse displayed towards her. Infuriatingly, she found herself wondering what Randall would do.

The patient in cubicle four was an ashen-faced girl in her twenties. There was a rough pressure-dressing covering the index finger of her left hand.

'How did you do it?' Kelly asked, as she gently picked the girl's hand up.

'Chopping up a cucumber—I'm a chef. Can you sew it back on, Doctor?'

'How long ago did this happen?'

'Only about ten minutes. My boss brought me by car straight away.'

Kelly took a look at the severed tip of finger. 'Well, you've done the right thing by bringing it in, and so promptly. I'm going to get hold of the surgeon right now, and hear what he says.'

She had him bleeped.

'Seton here,' came the clipped, deep voice.

Kelly took a deep breath. 'Hello, Randall—it's Kelly.'

There was a pause. 'Yes, Kelly?' he said indifferently. 'What can I do for you?'

'I've got a young girl in Casualty who's chopped off the tip of her finger. I think you might be able to sew it back on. Any chance of doing it now?'

'I'll come down and have a look, and tack her on to the front of my list if I think it's viable.'

'Thanks.'

'OK.' He hung up abruptly, and Kelly tried to convince herself that she didn't care.

She saw him only briefly when he came into the office to pick up the casualty card from the desk at which she was working. She glanced up with an automatic smile, her face stiffening as he threw her a look of sheer indifference. Yes, she had told him she didn't want him in her life, but was there really any need for him to be quite so unpleasant about it?

Her face was pink with anger as she finished filling in an X-ray form, and she was glad enough of the diversion when she was called to examine a five-year-old boy who had a skin tear to his forearm.

He was screaming his head off even before Kelly had gone near him.

'Ssssh!' urged Kelly softly, as she walked over to the trolley. 'What's your name?'

'Go *away*!' he retorted, and aimed a kick at Kelly's abdomen.

'No kicking, please, Caspian,' said Kelly firmly, reading his name off the casualty card. 'Start cleaning the wound so that I can examine it, would you please, Nurse?' She turned to the thin-faced woman in the green waxed jacket who sat beside him. 'Are you Caspian's mother?'

'Yes. Oh, Nurse, *please*,' the woman twittered, as the volume of Caspian's shrieks increased. 'He's a *very* sensitive child. Would you mind treating him more gently?'

'Nurse is trained to be gentle,' said Kelly smoothly. 'But it's bound to hurt a little bit. Tell me, is Caspian up to date with his tetanus injections?'

Caspian's mother looked appalled. '*Tetanus* injections?' she queried, in a shocked voice. 'Most certainly not! His father and I are not into *conventional* medicine, I'm afraid, Doctor.'

'Well, he's going to need a booster,' said Kelly firmly, as she peered down at Caspian's arm. 'It's a filthy wound.'

Caspian shrieked.

'And I'm going to have to suture his arm, I'm afraid,' said Kelly calmly. 'But I'll give him some local anaesthetic first, and he won't feel a thing.'

Pandemonium reigned as Caspian's mother passed out on hearing this, and hit her head on the side of the trolley. She then needed a skull X-ray and was put in the adjoining cubicle for neurological observations before being pronounced fit enough to go home.

'The only good thing about it,' laughed Kelly to the nurse in the office afterwards, 'was that the surprise of being upstaged by his mother actually shut dear Caspian up, so that I was able to stitch his arm without getting my eardrums shattered!'

The ringing of the telephone interrupted them, and Kelly picked up the receiver. 'Dr Hartley,' she said crisply.

It was Warren. 'Kelly?'

Kelly nearly dropped the phone. He had been the last person she would have expected to hear from after last night. 'Hello?' she answered cautiously.

'Can I see you?'

'I don't think that's a good idea.'

He hesitated. 'About last night. . .'

She froze. 'I don't really want to talk about it.'

'Will you——' he hesitated; he sounded nervous '—be taking any further action?'

Kelly swallowed. 'I've decided not to.'

'Thanks——'

Her voice was tinged with disgust as she cut him short. 'Don't thank me, Warren. I'm doing it to spare myself the humiliation of having to recount the whole sorry experience. But I know what you did, and so does Randall——'

'Oh, does he?' he sneered. 'Did Randall get lucky after I'd gone? Did you get laid?'

In a minute she would put the phone down, but not before he knew the strength of her resolve. 'Listen to me,' she said, very quietly, 'while I tell you that if ever there's a repeat of what happened last night, if I ever hear that you've tried something like that on with another woman, then I'll go straight to the police. And that's a promise.'

'Oh, don't worry, Kelly,' and there was an odd, strained quality to his voice. 'The situation won't arise again. You've taught me a lesson that I don't think I'll ever forget.'

But it was not relief which she felt as she replaced the receiver, and her hand trembled very slightly as she realised that she was unnerved and unsettled by the conversation she had just had, by the strange threatening tone in Warren's voice.

At six she finished her shift, taking the long way back to her room through the hospital gardens. She tried to relax, but the events of last night left her with a nasty taste in her mouth. Above her, the sky was the cloudless blue of late summer, and she knew that she could not face going back to her small, anonymous room in the doctors' mess. She needed to get out, just get away from the hospital.

On an impulse she took a bus to Hammersmith, and just over an hour later she found herself walking slowly up the dusty pavement towards her parents' house. The little terraced houses were tightly packed together, their windows masked by net curtains, though here and there Kelly could see that some of the old-fashioned front doors had been replaced by pine. There were even a few window-boxes, with blue lobelia and pink busy lizzies bravely blooming in spite of the dust which had coloured all the houses grey.

'Kelly!' Her mother opened the door with a surprised smile, and then a worried look crossed over her face. 'There's nothing wrong, is there?'

Kelly shook her head and grinned. 'No, of course not. Why should there be?'

'It's just that—well, you never really call without phoning.'

'I can go away again,' teased Kelly.

'Of course not! Come inside and I'll put the kettle on. Oh, it *is* nice to see you.'

Kelly stepped into the gloom of the narrow hallway. 'Where's Dad?'

'Guess!'

'At the pub?' Kelly hazarded, as she followed her mother into the old-fashioned kitchen.

Her mother nodded as she took her apron off and hung it over the back of the chair. 'But he's better than he used to be. Only has two at the most.' She paused. 'You'll never guess what he's done?' She put three teaspoons of tea into the warmed pot.

'What?'

'Given up smoking!'

'You're joking!'

'I'm not. That's all thanks to you, that is. The way you kept on to him about it. He says he feels much better for it too.' She handed Kelly a cup of the steaming, strong tea.

'You're looking very peaky yourself, dear. I can make you a bacon sandwich, if you like.'

Kelly hadn't eaten since toast at breakfast, and that seemed a very long time ago. 'I'd love one, Mum.'

Ten minutes later Kelly was eating the most delicious sandwich imaginable, with heaps of bacon layered between two doorsteps of buttered white bread. A dietician's nightmare, she thought in amusement. And a dieter's dream! 'Thanks, Mum,' she sighed, and put the empty plate down.

Her mother eyed her shrewdly. 'So are you going to tell me what's troubling you now?'

Kelly narrowed her eyes. 'How do you know that something's troubling me?'

'I can tell. You've got that look about you. It's something in the eyes—you've always done it—even as a little girl. It's not work, is it? Changed your mind about what you want to do again?'

Kelly sighed. 'No, it's not work. Well, in a way it's work.' She saw her mother's puzzled expression. 'It's a man,' she said.

'A man!'

Kelly pulled a face. 'Well, there's no need to sound so surprised, Mum! Lots of women have men worries.'

'But not you. You've never been interested in any men. Except for. . .'

Her voice tailed off. Kelly stared at her interestedly. 'Except for who?'

Her mother hesitated. 'The student. All those years ago. Had a funny name.'

'Randall.'

'Randall. That's right. Used to cry yourself to sleep every night after you got back from that summer camp.'

'He's back,' said Kelly slowly. 'Randall's back.'

Her mother listened. 'And you feel the same about him?'

Kelly thought carefully as she searched around for the honest answer to her mother's question. 'Yes,' she whispered softly. 'I do. Oh, I've tried to tell myself otherwise, that I don't, but—in my heart of hearts—he still means more to me than any other man I've ever met.'

Mrs Hartley's eyes narrowed. 'And? He's not interested?'

Kelly bit her lip. 'That's just the thing. I think— he is.'

'So what's the problem?'

'Years ago—all those years ago—Randall and I grew very fond of one another, but then the night before I was leaving, he. . .' She hesitated, not wanting to give too much away to her mother about how intimate they had almost become when she had been just seventeen. 'Walked out. And he went back to London. He never phoned me or contacted me. I never saw him again until the other day.' She put her teacup down. 'You see, he hurt me very badly,' she said.

'I know that.'

'And what sort of guarantee have I got that he won't do it again?'

Her mother shook her head. 'Unfortunately, life doesn't come with those kind of guarantees, Kelly. And relationships certainly don't. Otherwise we'd never make any mistakes. But, while playing cautious is always the safe option, it's not always the best option.'

Kelly recognised the wisdom in her mother's words as she twisted her hands in her lap. She realised too that this was the first time she had ever confided in her, and in thinking that she would not understand she had done her mother a great disservice all these years. 'There's something else I haven't told you, Mum.'

'And what's that, dear?'

How could she say it? 'Randall—he's. . .' Heavens—it sounded so ridiculously pretentious; it sounded unreal. 'He's. . . Well, he's a lord, actually. His name's Lord Rousay.'

Her mother looked momentarily abashed, then nodded. 'So?'

Kelly's mouth fell open in astonishment; her family was being full of surprises this afternoon. Her father had given up smoking, and now her mother was calmly accepting Randall's aristocratic status as though she were being confronted with this kind of problem all the time! She shrugged her slim shoulders. 'It's a bit like the prince and the showgirl, don't you think? Him and me?'

'No, I don't. You're a doctor and so is he, that's equal enough. And from what you tell me, you seem to like each other—so that's really all that matters.'

Kelly laughed aloud. 'I thought you'd. . .'

Her mother's eyes twinkled. 'Tell you that you were getting ideas above your station? If I'd believed that, we'd never have supported your ambition to be a doctor in the first place. I would have liked your opportunities myself.' She sighed as she poured them both another cup of tea. 'But things were different in our day.'

'You mean you didn't want to leave school at fourteen?'

Her mother gave her a funny look. 'Of course I didn't! But we needed the money, and when I say *needed* it, I mean it. There were no grants around in my day.'

'I was very lucky,' said Kelly in a low voice, deeply moved by what her mother had just told her, aware that to a teenager everything seemed so black and white, which was not always necessarily the case. She would never have imagined for a moment that her mother would have liked to go on to further education. 'Thank you for everything.'

Her mother beamed with pleasure. 'We're very proud of you, Kelly, don't sell yourself short. If he's not bothered about the differences between you, then why should you be?' She hesitated. 'You say he just walked out of your life?'

Kelly nodded.

'And did you never ask him why?'

She shook her head, so that the auburn hair rippled in fiery waves all the way down her back. 'No.'

'Then why don't you?'

Kelly's eyes widened. 'I couldn't do that!' she protested.

'Then you aren't being fair,' said Mrs Hartley firmly.

'You mean to him?'

Mrs Hartley shook her head. 'Not to him. To yourself.'

Kelly stared into space, her green eyes troubled.

'Perhaps I'm not,' she murmured slowly, thinking what a simple solution it was, yet wondering if she had the nerve simply to confront Randall and ask him outright why he had left her.

CHAPTER SIX

KELLY thought and thought about what her mother had said, about asking Randall for an explanation.

Of course she had not asked him why he had walked out on her all those years ago. He had had nine years to find her if there had been a reasonable explanation, and he hadn't bothered. And now he was back, and obviously still as attracted to her as she was to him, probably thinking that if she was as compliant as she had been before, that he might as well have an affair with her.

An affair which would bring her nothing but heartache.

So what was the alternative to an affair? Was it possible that they could bury desire, and become, if not best buddies, then at least friends?

But you could not be friends with a man who was frostily polite to you, who deliberately excluded you from his life as Randall now seemed to be doing, as he so crushingly demonstrated one day in A & E.

Kelly was standing behind the curtains of a cubicle, trying to get a history from a woman who spoke only French, when she heard Randall talking to his houseman outside the cubicle.

'Come and have a drink later in the mess—there are a few people coming.'

'What's the occasion?'

'My birthday.' Randall's voice was wry. 'Not the venue I'd normally have chosen for such an auspicious occasion, but—typically—I'm on call.'

'Your birthday, Mr Seton?'

Kelly cringed as she heard heard Staff Nurse Higgs' syrupy tones.

'That's right.'

'I just *love* birthdays,' cooed Nurse Higgs.

Kelly bristled as she heard the indulgent tone in Randall's voice. 'Want to come for a drink in the mess later?'

'Just try to stop me!'

Kelly felt sick. He could have gone out with *anyone*. Surely he was not going to start dating the awful staff nurse who made being obvious into an art form!

'*Docteur! Docteur! J'ai mal au ventre! C'est terrible, Docteur!*' The woman on the trolley was gripping Kelly's hand tightly. And then she slipped into a torrent of totally incomprehensible French.

'*Attend, s'il vous plaît*,' stumbled Kelly in her absolutely appalling schoolgirl French. '*Je trouverai une personne qui. . .*'

'Having problems?' came a deep drawl from close by, and the curtains were swished back to disclose Randall, his grey eyes resting innocently on her flushed face.

Fancy blushing like an idiotic schoolgirl! 'I need a fluent French speaker to take this patient's full history,' she said stiltedly.

'Will I do?' he drawled.

It was little things in life that could rile you so

much that you felt like screaming. Like the fact that he had invited everyone for a drink except her. And that the arrogant show-off just *happened* to be fluent in French!

'Only if you have the time,' she said stiffly.

'*Bien sûr!*' he mocked, and leaned over the patient. '*Bonjour, madame.*' He lapsed into flawless French with an impeccable accent, while the patient virtually fainted with pleasure at the sight of the tall Englishman with the spectacular dark-lashed eyes who was speaking her language with such fluid ease.

Angrily, Kelly turned to leave.

He lifted his head, some unreadable light in the depths of the steely eyes. 'Won't you stay to chaperon me?'

'I'll send a nurse instead,' she said tartly. 'I'm sure that Nurse Higgs would be only too *delighted* to assist you.'

As soon as the words were out, she regretted them, and she didn't need the quirk of amusement which lifted the corners of his mouth to tell her that she had succeeded in sounding jealous. How *could* she have done?

'I'm sure you're right,' he murmured, still smiling, his fingers lightly resting on the patient's pulse.

Kelly walked back into the office, where Nurse Higgs was perched on the edge of the desk, chatting to the houseman and swinging her shapely legs like a pendulum. 'Would you mind going to assist Mr Seton, please, Nurse?'

Nurse Higgs wriggled her bottom off the desk, her look of rapture quickly being replaced by one of

triumph. 'I'd be delighted,' she purred, then added
to the houseman, 'See you tonight, then, Damian,
at *Randall's* party.' She couldn't resist a triumphant
glance over at Kelly, but Kelly lowered her head and
doggedly carried on writing on the casualty card.

She wouldn't let it bother her, she just wouldn't.
He could go out with whom he liked, and they were
welcome to him. She, for one, was well rid of him.

With a determination to put Randall out of her
mind, Kelly picked up a set of notes which were
awaiting the arrival of a GP admission, and began to
read them.

She managed to lose herself in them so completely
that she didn't hear Joe, the male nurse, come in
until he cleared his throat and grinned at her.

Kelly looked up and smiled back. Joe was in his
mid-forties, and the longest-serving member of the
casualty staff. 'Hi,' she said. 'Got something for me?'

Joe nodded. 'A young woman with acute, severe
abdominal pain.'

Something in the way he said it made Kelly give
him a sharp look. 'But?'

Joe hesitated. 'There's something you should
know.'

'Mmm?'

'She's known to us. She's given a false name, but
I recognised her. She's in our black book.'

'Oh. I see,' said Kelly slowly.

The black book.

Most casualty departments reluctantly kept one.
In it they listed persistent abusers of the system,

such as drug addicts and faked illness in order to obtain strong painkillers.

'What's she in the black book for, Joe?' Kelly asked quietly.

He pulled a face. 'Münchhausen.'

'Oh,' said Kelly again as she followed Joe towards the cubicle, her mind scanning over what she knew about Münchhausen's Syndrome. She'd read about it, naturally, but this was the first case of it she'd actually encountered in four months of working in A & E.

Named after Baron von Münchhausen—proverbial teller of tall stories—Münchhausen's Syndrome was a disturbing psychiatric disorder of unknown aetiology. Patients became addicted to hospitals, and to hospital treatment. Hospitals somehow gave their usually miserable lives some meaning and importance. In a bizarre form of attention-seeking, they often endured many major surgical interventions before their condition was diagnosed.

Kelly pulled the curtains open and looked at the overweight and pasty young woman who lay doubled up on the trolley.

'Hello,' she said gently, as she put her fingers on the girl's wrist. 'What seems to be the trouble?'

The girl was hyperventilating. 'Just give me something for the pain!' she gasped. 'Please, Doctor!'

'You'll have to try and give me a bit of your history,' said Kelly quietly.

'I've got Crohn's disease, but this pain is worse than anything I've ever had before! I feel like it's going to kill me, Doctor! For God's sake, can't you give me something for the pain?'

Kelly shook her head. 'I can't give you anything just yet. I need to examine you first. Now will you show me exactly where the pain is?'

'Here,' the girl muttered, and as she lifted her arm to point to her abdomen, Kelly caught sight of the tell-tale multiple scarring on her wrists which indicated self-mutilation.

Kelly examined her. Her abdomen was covered in old scars, and the list of operations she cited was truly astonishing. Eventually, Kelly straightened up. I'm going to ask a specialist to come down and take a look at you,' she said, and indicated to Joe that he should follow her.

Back in the office, she frowned. 'I don't *think* there's anything physically wrong with her. Her abdomen is certainly rigid, but I got the feeling that she was controlling that herself by holding her breath. And if she *has* Crohn's disease, then the level of pain she was demonstrating would be indicative of a perforation, but her observations certainly didn't tally with *that*. It's a psychiatric referral we need,' she said, in a low voice. 'But we need to get hold of her notes, and I'd better get her checked out by the general surgeon just in case. This might just be the first genuine medical crisis of her life, and I'm not prepared to take that risk.'

She bleeped Randall, who said he would be down straight away, and, true to his word, he appeared almost immediately.

'How sure are we it's Münchhausen?' he asked Kelly.

'Pretty sure. Her wrists and abdomen are riddled with scars. Joe recognised her immediately. She has a history of visiting this department, using various aliases. I've sent for her notes, but of course there may be more than one set floating around.' She lifted her eyes to his. 'But I have to be sure that she doesn't have a *genuine* surgical problem before I can give her a psychiatric referral.'

'Sure.' Randall nodded, took the casualty card from her and went off with Joe to examine the patient, but he had returned within minutes, a rueful expression on his face.

'She's gone,' he said succinctly.

'Gone?' Kelly frowned.

'Mmm. Done a runner, as they say. She obviously guessed that you suspected her.'

'That was pretty stupid of me!' Kelly threw her pen down on the desk crossly. 'How on earth can we help her if she goes off like that?'

Randall gave her a curiously sympathetic look. 'But you know that we can't help her anyway, Kelly, not if she doesn't want to help herself.' And he gave her a brief smile before he turned and was gone.

Kelly was absolutely exhausted by the time her shift had finished, but the prospect of an evening alone didn't fill her with joy, particularly if she had to play witness to the sound of the tip-tapping of feet as they wended their way to Randall's birthday drinks in the mess.

She decided to ring the hospital squash club, and

luckily found herself a partner for that evening, a girl called Penny, one of the nursing sisters from ITU, whom Kelly had partnered on a number of occasions.

Kelly played a vigorous game but was completely thrashed, and afterwards, both panting for breath, they shook hands.

'You weren't concentrating!' scolded Penny, her face all pink and shiny. 'You're normally much better than me! Not that I'm complaining,' she added, with a grin. 'I really enjoyed winning!' She rubbed a towel at the back of her neck. 'What are you doing now? Anything?'

Kelly shrugged. 'I hadn't planned anything.'

Penny's eyes narrowed. 'You've split up with Warren Booth, haven't you?'

Kelly had to try very hard not to shudder at the mention of his name; she had managed very successfully to put the memories of Warren completely out of her mind. 'Yes,' she said. 'We have. But it actually wasn't serious.'

Penny laughed. 'That's not what the gossip said. Rumour has it that Warren was seen prowling around jewellers' shop windows at the dead of night!'

God forbid, thought Kelly, wondering how she could have been so blind and so insensitive as not to have seen that he was so keen on her.

Penny zipped her squash racquet into its case. 'Well, if you're free, do you fancy coming for a drink? There's a crowd going down to the doctors' mess.'

'No, thanks, I——' The automatic words of refusal froze on Kelly's lips as she realised what had prompted them, and indignation reared its head. This was *her* hospital, after all. She had trained here, worked here since qualifying. And she *did* quite fancy a drink after a hard day's work and her game of squash. So was she going to let her confused feelings about Randall change her life to such an extent that she could no longer even go out for a friendly drink with a girlfriend?

'Actually, yes,' she amended quickly. 'I'd love to.'

'Great! Shall I meet you there in about half an hour?' asked Penny. 'That gives us time for a shower, and to slap a bit of make-up on.'

'Fine. See you there.'

Kelly showered and dressed simply in a pair of old jeans worn with a simple emerald-coloured body, which brought out the deep green of her eyes, but her nerve almost failed her as she stood outside the mess, listening to the raised voices of laughter which were coming from inside.

There was a split-second silence when she walked in, and then there were shouts of 'hello' from several people who knew her.

She knew exactly where Randall stood in the room, and though she heard him talking, laughing, she immediately became aware that his attention was fixed on her. The grey eyes were following her with their intense, spectacular gaze, and that knowledge filled her with a heady excitement which was immediately dampened down when her gaze came to rest by chance on Nurse Higgs.

Marianne Higgs was looking stunning. Her silky blonde hair streamed all over her magnificent bosom, and she was wearing a short, tight T-shirt dress which showed a great deal of bare, brown thighs. But it was her coldly hostile look which unnerved Kelly, and she shook her head a little to dispel a sudden, irrational fear. Because for a moment there, the other girl had glowered at her as though she really despised her.

'Hello, Kelly,' said Penny, who had appeared by her side.

Kelly forced her attention back to her squash partner. 'Hi!' she said. 'Feeling better for that shower?'

'You bet!' Penny looked at her and gave a rueful smile. 'How on earth can you look so good just wearing a pair of jeans and a body? Half the room can't keep their eyes off you.'

Kelly shook her head, and the auburn waves rippled down her back. 'You look great too.'

Penny looked down at her flower-sprigged dress. 'I'm much too short and curvy. I certainly couldn't get away with wearing *that* outfit!'

'Some men like curvy women,' smiled Kelly.

'So they tell me. I'm still waiting to meet them! Come on, let's get a drink. Loser pays!'

'OK,' laughed Kelly, and they walked up to the bar.

They bought two glasses of beer and Kelly reached into the back pocket of her jeans for some money.

'It's already paid for,' came a deep voice behind her.

Her heart began its wild and familiar dance. She turned round slowly to face him, almost drowning in the dazzle of that grey, speculative stare. Suddenly it was difficult to speak. 'You—don't have to do that.' Did her voice sound hesitant, stumbling?

'It's my pleasure,' he insisted, with a smile.

Aware that Penny was standing silently by her side, Kelly quickly turned to her squash partner. 'Do you two know each other?'

Penny's eyes were fixed on him with frank admiration. 'Oh, yes, I know Randall,' she said, sipping her drink. 'He's a regular face in ITU. I think I could quite like him if he didn't send us so many patients! Thanks for the drink, Randall—cheers!' and she lifted her glass up to him.

He raised his mineral water in silent toast and then the cool grey eyes were turned on Kelly.

With an effort she lifted her glass to him, hostility and the years forgotten as she lost herself in that devastating smile. 'Happy birthday,' she said in a quiet voice, hardly realising that she had said it.

The dark eyebrows were elevated. 'Why, thank you, Kelly,' he murmured, and an undercurrent of sardonic amusement transmitted its way towards her. 'But I wasn't aware that you knew it was my birthday?'

Of course he wasn't—because she had been shamelessly eavesdropping at the time! Of all the crass things to do! 'I—er, er—overheard you telling someone earlier.'

He was staring very deliberately at her mouth, as

though he wanted very much to kiss it, and Kelly put her glass down with a hand that was in terrible danger of trembling.

Penny was looking from one to the other of them with a bemused expression on her face. 'I think I'm a little *de trop* here,' she said drily, and then, with an obvious sigh of relief, 'Oh, look, there's some people from ITU, you must excuse me. Great game, Kelly, thanks!'

'Let's do it again soon,' said Kelly from between parched lips, as she watched Penny go. 'I must go too, Randall.'

'Don't.' He put his hand at the small of her back, at the most delicious spot, as though he were about to massage it, and she had physically to force herself not to wriggle back against it luxuriously.

'I haven't eaten.' Her voice sounded strange, even to her own ears. As though she had forgotten how to speak, because the dryness of her mouth and the blood thundering to her temples was utterly distracting.

'Neither have I. We'll get a Chinese meal delivered, if you'd like it.'

'Randall?'

His voice was very soft. 'What?'

'I must go. I don't know why I came.'

'Yes, you do,' he demurred. 'It's pointless fighting it any more, Kelly. It's inevitable.'

He made it sound as though they were doomed; doomed to be swept away into a mad sea of their own passion, and she wondered whether they would sink, or swim.

'Come and have some champagne with me?' he suggested.

'In your room, I suppose?' she answered bitterly.

'Well, yes.' He sighed. 'Hell—don't look like that! I happen to be on call, so I can't leave the hospital, which leaves us with a number of alternatives. We can postpone this talk which we're long overdue to have until tomorrow night, but frankly, you're so damned elusive that I'm extremely reluctant to do that.'

'And don't I get a say in all this?' she countered, but her breathing was erratic.

'Only if you agree with me,' he said softly.

She stared at him, momentarily flummoxed and rendered speechless by his effrontery, his flattery.

'So,' he continued, still in that deep, seductive drawl, 'we can stay here where everything is getting rowdier by the second. . .'

Kelly glanced up, frozen once again in the malicious ice which glittered from Marianne Higgs' eyes. No, she certainly did not want to stay here.

'Or we can do the sensible thing, and go some-where quiet to talk——'

'Like the hospital canteen, I suppose?' she put in drily. 'Or the library?'

He gave her a sweet smile and a feeling like a flock of butterflies tumbled about exultantly in the pit of her stomach. 'Perhaps not private enough,' he murmured, and there was no disguising the sensual glimmer which lay behind the question in the silver-grey eyes.

She tried to tell herself that it was because she wanted to straighten things out between them, but if

she put her hand across her heart she knew that was
not the reason. The reason was love—plain and
simple. She'd loved Randall at seventeen, and she
had never stopped loving him. There had never been
another man to match him for wit, or charm, or
charisma or irresistible sex appeal.

She would ask him why he had left, and if the
answer he gave her did not satisfy her—then she
would walk away and never look back. Because she
would never respect herself if she did anything
different.

She became aware of the hostile daggers of
Marianne Higgs' glance. 'But won't I be cramping
your style?' she enquired, somewhat waspishly.

'What?' And he saw the staff nurse looking over
at them.

'Oh, I see. No, of course you won't.'

'There's no "of course" about it. She's glaring
over here as though I'm poaching on her territory.'

'Well, you're not, and forgive me for saying so,
Kelly—but *you're* the one who is sounding a trifle
put out. One might almost say jealous?'

'I'm not jealous,' she whispered, wondering if he
could read the lie in her eyes.

'I think we're rather going round in circles here,'
he said softly. 'So are you coming with me, or not?'

Nine years on and she had become a strong,
independent woman in everything. Except this.
Him. 'Yes,' she sighed.

He grimaced. 'There's no need to sound as though
I'm leading you into a den of lions.'

'Probably safer,' she retorted.

He laughed. 'No comment. Wait here while I go and tell them to leave a tab at the bar.'

'That's very expansive of you,' she commented.

'Oh, but I'm feeling very expansive—quite extraordinarily so,' he murmured, and his gaze travelled lingeringly all the way down her body, causing her to tremble helplessly under that slow, seductive scrutiny.

He strode over to the bar, his tall, rangy dark figure attracting the attention of every woman in the room.

Oh, this is hopeless, thought Kelly. He's a walking dream-machine. Elusive and gorgeous—and who in their right mind could ever expect to hang on to Randall Seton?

'Everyone's watching us,' she observed, when he came back from the bar.

'Of course they are. All the men are envious as hell of me, and all the women are wishing they looked as beautiful as you do tonight.'

'Don't try to flatter me.'

'I'm not,' he smiled. 'I pride myself on a candid tongue.'

Compliments from Randall could turn a girl's head, and she forced herself to be prosaic. 'And it'll be all round the hospital tomorrow.'

He was staring at her very intently. 'What will?'

'Us. If we leave together.'

'And do you mind?'

She stared into the dark, handsome face which had haunted her dreams and her waking hours for so many years, and realised that no, she *didn't* mind.

More than that—Kelly felt almost reckless with an anticipation and excitement she had not tasted for years.

'No,' she answered quietly, 'I don't think I do.'

She waved goodbye to Penny, and walked out of the room, with Randall following closely behind her, but she was aware of the excited buzz of chatter as they left. They walked in silence along the corridor to his room, and she found herself wondering how she would view her recklessness in the morning.

He shut the door behind her and she half expected him to pull her into his arms and kiss her, but he didn't. Instead he walked to the opposite side of the room, away from her, and gestured towards the fridge. 'Champagne?' he asked, and he sounded almost distracted.

'I thought you said that you were on call.'

'I am. I'm not having any—but you can.'

'Don't open a bottle just for me.'

'Oh, for God's sake!' he exploded, and his face was a mask of tight, angry lines. 'Nine years of wanting and waiting and we're standing making inane comments about what we are or what we're not drinking, like two people who've just met at a cocktail party!'

She found his savagery exciting, perplexing, but disturbing too. She realised suddenly, for the first time, that deep, dark, angry emotions ran beneath the outwardly urbane sophistication which was Randall's trademark. She did not know what she had expected when she came here tonight, but it had certainly not been anger. 'Perhaps I'd better go,' she

said curtly. 'You brought the subject up, after all.
You offered me champagne, but I don't really care
if I have any of not. I was under the impression that
you wanted to talk. However, if you *don't* want to
talk——'

'No,' he whispered, and his eyes glittered with
dark, devastating fire. 'You're quite right—I don't
want to talk, Kelly, In fact, talking's the last thing
on my mind right now. Because I want to make love
to you. All night long, and every other night of my
life. You must know how much I want you, Kelly.
How badly.'

She felt her body react instantly to the raw passion
in his words. She felt the hot sweetness of desire,
the full flooding to her breasts as he spoke.

'You *do* know that, don't you, Kelly?' His voice
shuddered on a sigh, but still, to her surprise, he had
not moved. And thank God he hadn't—for after
that stark avowal of need that had thrilled her to the
core of her body, would she have been able to resist
him if he had come to her; taken her into his arms;
kissed away her doubts and replaced them with fire
and with passion?

She sat down in an armchair and made her mind
focus on one of the water-colours on the wall. It was
not hospital issue; he had obviously brought it with
him. There were several more by the same artist.
She liked them very much, and then she saw, with a
tearing wrench of her heart, that one depicted his
family home. Seton House.

He followed the direction of her gaze, then let his
eyes fall on her white cheeks, her widened eyes. He

came to kneel at her feet, to take both small frozen hands in his own.

'Yes, I know,' he said. 'That beautiful summer.'

But the tears, refusing to be suppressed any longer, had risen up in her throat, sparkling saltily in her big green eyes. She forced the question, knowing that if it was never asked, then any future with Randall would stop right here.

'Why did you leave me like that, Randall?'

His mouth twisted, as though he were in pain, as he expelled a breath of air on a long, long sigh. 'Because I was in love with you——'

His words made her so angry that she tried to get out of the chair, but he would not let her; the firm pressure of his hands was just too restricting.

'Don't lie to me,' she said huskily, a tear trickling down her cheek. 'Say what you want, but don't lie to me. I haven't come here to listen to your lies.'

He frowned. 'It was no lie. You knew how I felt about you. Everyone did—it was as obvious as life itself. And I knew what you felt about me——'

'Oh, yes,' she interrupted bitterly. 'You loved me so much that you ran off and left, without a word to say why.'

'But don't you realise why?' he asked softly.

'No. I don't.'

He glanced down at her hands, enclosed so warmly in his, then looked up into her face again. 'Let me tell you then, Kelly. I'd met hundreds of beautiful women in my life, but at twenty-four no one had ever remotely touched my heart. And then I saw you, and. . .' He gave a slow smile as he remembered. 'For someone who bordered on cynicism, who didn't believe in love at first sight, it came as something of a shock to me. Because when I saw you, that was it. Lights, stars, fireworks—the whole business.' He paused, as if searching for the right words. 'But everything was against it, us——'

'You mean that I wasn't an Honourable-some-thing-or-other?' she put in caustically.

He shook his head. 'Darling, I really don't care about my title; I never have. Most of the time it's been a hindrance instead of a help—and certainly in medicine it's done me no favours at all. I told you. People tend to have preconceptions about you. Some women find it a turn-on, but how could a man respect a woman who was interested in him solely because he happened to have a title?'

'Which, presumably, was why you didn't tell me about it at first?'

He frowned. 'You know what the reason was. Not because I thought that it would attract you. I knew as soon as I looked into those beautiful big green eyes, that you weren't the kind of girl to be influenced one way or another. I didn't tell you because I didn't want you be intimidated by it—it *can* be intimidating,' he emphasised. 'And that *isn't* supposed to be patronising. I wanted one afternoon with you where all we needed to be were the people we really were. Underneath.

'And we had it. If I thought I'd fallen in love with you when you stood so wide-eyed and gorgeous carrying that ridiculous old suitcase, then I was certain after I'd spent the afternoon with you.' He shook his head slowly as he remembered. 'You were so bright and so passionate and so sweet. Very, very sweet. Unaffected.'

She let her eyelids flutter down to hide the confusion and the suggestion of tears which still threatened to fall, touched by the poignancy of his words, reluctant to let herself believe them.

'When I said I wanted to see you again, I meant it. I imagined us going out together while you went through medical school. And then, that night, when we almost made love, you said something which completely freaked me out.'

She stared at him in confusion, racking her brain to know what he meant. 'What?'

'You said, "You won't make me pregnant, will you?" Don't you remember?'

Yes. Come to think of it, she did remember. She had been haunted by a vision of someone she had been to school with, prematurely old and pushing a pram. 'Yes,' she affirmed. 'I remember. But——'

'It brought me to my senses,' he said savagely. 'And how! I thought about what we'd so nearly done. You'd told me all about your struggles to get your study taken seriously, how difficult it had been to persuade your parents to let you go to university, when none of your friends were going. I thought of all the sacrifices that they had probably had to make; would continue to have to make. And here was I, supposed to be a responsible medical student. Yet I almost made love to you, unprotected, without a thought for the consequences, because I was enraptured by you, so crazy for you. With a single act, we could have put your career to death before it had even begun. Didn't you realise that?'

'But that doesn't explain why you left without a word of explanation. We could have. . .' Her voice tailed off.

He understood immediately. 'Yes, we could have sorted out some contraception. We could have followed my original plan and continued to see one another when we were both back in London. But. . .'

'But?' she prompted, and she was now no longer afraid to look him in the eyes; something in his voice told her unequivocally that the words he spoke were true.

'I knew that if we did, the chances of it lasting were small. All the odds were against us. You were still at school; I was working hard at medical school. Romance would get in the way of study—not just yours, but mine too. And then I would have qualified, perhaps been sent to a hospital miles away, working a one-in-two, giving us little opportunity to spend time together. I could see all those things whittling away at our relationship, and I didn't want to risk it. You see, it was too precious to me. You were too precious to me, and I simply didn't want to risk losing you.'

Kelly felt some languorous flame of relief invade her body, like sweetest fire. 'Don't stop now,' she urged as he fell silent, the grey eyes studying her intently.

He gave her a sad smile. 'And so I decided to let you do what you'd always wanted to do—to succeed as a doctor, without bringing any undue pressures to bear on you. And then, only then, would I come back to find you.' He frowned. 'Kelly. Don't you realise that it wasn't just coincidence that brought me here to St Christopher's? I came here to find *you.*'

He had missed out on an obvious point of logic.

'But what if I'd met someone else along the way?'

He shrugged. 'That was a risk I had to take.' Then he gave her a wickedly arrogant smile. 'I was pretty sure you wouldn't.'

Her mouth twitched. 'What an ego!' she whispered in mock disbelief; but he was right and, what was more, he knew he was right. 'And what about you? What if you'd found someone else?'

His eyes were very soft. 'I knew I wouldn't.'

'Oh, Randall,' she said helplessly.

'What?'

Her mouth curved into a totally new and over-whelmingly exciting smile, that of a woman who had rediscovered her sensuality, and was about to have it awakened. 'Let's go to bed,' she whispered.

He murmured something sweet, profound and essentially shocking beneath his breath, and the raw words thrilled her. 'Kelly—you are an amazing woman, do you know that?' But he did not wait for her answer as he pulled her to her feet, put his arms round her and kissed her with a passion so intense that she felt she could die from the heady pleasure of it.

'Oh, my darling,' he whispered against her mouth.

'Do you know how many nights I've dreamed of this moment?'

'Yes,' she sighed helplessly, all reasoned thought deserting her as her fingers reached up to coil themselves in the thick waves of his dark hair, then fell to rest possessively on the broad, powerful breadth of his shoulders. 'Oh, yes!'

His hand immediately slipped the body down from her shoulders to cup and smooth her bare breast with shocking and devastating intimacy as though he could not wait to caress her naked skin, but she did not care—they had both waited far too long for this—and she didn't want to wait a second longer. She wanted him now. Right now.

She began to tug impatiently at his tie, when a deafening alarm echoed through the room. They both froze in horrified disbelief as his emergency bleep shrilled with its persistent and ear-splitting sound from the pocket of his white coat.

CHAPTER SEVEN

'*HELL*!' exploded Randall, and swore softly and explicitly beneath his breath, but with an effort he got his breath back and picked up the telephone immediately, giving Kelly a rueful and frustrated glance as he waited.

She brushed her hand back through her ruffled hair, her own pulse starting to slow down to normal as she gazed on the ruffled black splendour of his hair, and the way that his tie was all awry. Oh, God—how she loved him!

'Seton here,' he said, then listened.

Kelly could see at once that whatever he was being bleeped for was serious, because he slammed the receiver down in its cradle and headed for the door. 'Sorry, darling,' he said swiftly. 'They're bringing an RTA into A & E.'

The shorthand of hospitals, so familiar. RTA— road traffic accident—one of the more horrific abbreviations. Kelly winced. 'Bad?'

He nodded, his expression tight. 'It seems so. Four teenagers. The fire brigade are cutting them out now.'

'Oh, God.' Realising from the way he was looking at her that she was still in a state of partial undress, Kelly glanced down and immediately pulled the body back up over her naked breasts, her eyebrows creased together in a frown as she realised that, because it was a week night, there would only be one casualty officer on duty. And that meant that there would be insufficient cover if the accident was really bad.

'You go on down,' she said to Randall briefly. 'I'll get my coat. I might as well come and help.'

'OK.' He gave her a brief, warm smile before he was gone, and then she ran out of his room and into her own, slipping into a sweater and some flat, comfortable shoes and quickly pulling on her white coat.

She ran down the corridor to A & E. For once running was permissible, since the old hospital rule still carried: Never run except in cases of fire or haemorrhage—and with four kids being cut out of a car by the fire brigade, there was sure to be haemorrhage. . .

Kelly arrived in the department, which seemed abnormally quiet, and the first person she saw was Harry Wells—automatically in charge of the department since he was the casualty officer on duty.

'I've come to help,' she said immediately.

He nodded. 'Randall told me.'

'What do you want me to do?'

'We're waiting for the ambulances to get here. Can you see if the night sister has arrived yet, and ask her to organise some extra nurses? We're going to need someone to cope with relatives. Then come and help deal with the casualties.'

'OK,' said Kelly. She sped off and relayed Harry's message to the duty night sister who had just arrived.

'It's going to be pretty bloody in there, so make sure that the relatives are kept well away, won't you, Sister?' she said quietly. 'And could you ask the receptionist to put out an announcement that all minor injuries may have to wait some time?'

'Sure. You can bet that all the minor injuries will be up in arms, though,' said the night sister cynically.

Then Kelly went swiftly back towards the resuscitation room just as the eerie blue light heralded the arrival of the first ambulance, and she immediately ran forward to join a small group of doctors who were at the door to greet it, stopping when they saw the expression on the ambulance man's face.

His face was white with an almost sickly green tinge, the sombre expression in his eyes conveying some of the horror he must have witnessed that night. And suddenly Kelly realised that the accident was very bad. Ambulance drivers were among the bravest and hardest working of the paramedics. The things they saw would make most people sleepless for a month. Kelly knew this particular officer too. He had been on the job for almost a decade, with a reputation for being calm and unflappable. And yet tonight he looked as shocked and appalled as the newest recruit.

'Who's the casualty officer?' he said blankly, and Randall and the others began to move away, aware of what was coming next.

Harry stepped forward. 'I am.'

'There's a. . .' His voice tailed off. He swallowed. 'DOA in the back. If you could. . .certify her, Doctor—then I can take the body straight down to the morgue. I feel I should warn you that. . .' His voice lowered; he looked around, as though afraid that relatives might be within earshot, even though he knew that all relatives were banned from this area of the department. 'She's been decapitated.' His voice broke then. 'Only about seventeen, and she's been decapitated.'

Harry went straight out and climbed into the back of the ambulance, and Kelly instinctively put an arm on the driver's shoulder. He was shaking quite badly. 'Go and get some tea,' she urged, 'after you've driven to the morgue. Don't go out on the roads until you've had something for shock. Do you understand?'

'Yes, Doctor,' he mumbled, like a polite child, and went back to his waiting vehicle.

And then came the sickening cacophony of noise which meant that more than one ambulance was pounding its way towards them.

After that it was mayhem and afterwards Kelly was only able to recall fragments of the long night.

People running around. People calling urgently to one another as trolleys with blood-stained sheets were being brought in.

Perhaps an outside observer might have found it all fragmented and disorganised, but every doctor and every nurse was rallying together as they had all been taught, to work at full stretch, with only the most essential words being spoken.

As Kelly helped push a trolley into the resuscitation room, she could see that already two grim-faced policemen stood, waiting for the all-clear from the doctors before they could interview any of the passengers.

Kelly looked down at the stretcher as they ran, trying to assess visually any obvious injuries before she had the chance to examine the patient. Amid the long, tangled hair and the caked blood she could see a girl of painfully tender years. She looked barely sixteen, her face almost colourless, the eyes closed, but with the strange, indefinable cast which differentiated sleep from unconsciousness. Kelly's face paled as she saw the crimson flowering of blood spreading ever wider on the sheet.

They bundled her into the large room, just as another trolley was brought in close behind.

'Over here, please!' Kelly said to the porter, and together they pushed the trolley into a spare space. Randall was already in there bending over another trolley, his houseman and a nurse by his side, all working urgently, their faces intent, disturbed.

The night charge nurse came straight over to Kelly's trolley. 'Can you do her observations, please,' she said, automatically pulling on a pair of latex gloves, since they all had it drummed into them night and day not to expose themselves to possible infection by blood.

Although the situation was grave, it was also very simple. In an emergency of this type, only the bare essentials of life-saving were relevant. It was necessary to maintain a clear airway, to stop haemorrhaging, and to replace the volume of fluid already lost before the body went into irreversible shock.

'Have the crash team been bleeped?' called Kelly.

'They're on their way,' someone called back.

At that moment, an anaesthetist from the crash team arrived. 'Someone else is on their way—who needs me most?'

'I do!' called Kelly. 'This girl needs intubating.' She allowed him access to the patient's head, and meanwhile she stripped the sheet off to seek the source of the blood. It was not difficult. Immediately a great red gush pumped out of a long gash in the arm, its bright colour and the force at which it was expelled meaning that it could only come from an artery.

'Get me some suction and an artery clip,' said Kelly quickly. 'And can someone else try and find a vein to get a line in?'

By now the rest of the crash team had arrived, and behind them, the orthopaedic team. The room was bursting with people.

'Any fractures?' called the orthopaedic registrar.

The charge nurse working with Kelly nodded. 'Here,' he said. 'Her leg's lying at an awkward angle.'

The orthopod strode over and ran his gaze over the limb with an experienced eye. 'Classic compound tib and fib,' he muttered. 'How's her general state?'

'Not brilliant,' admitted Kelly, as she pushed the suction catheter out of the way. 'She's lost a lot of fluid and—oh, *good*—I've got the clip on! Now let's get some fluid into her, and can we do some neuro obs on her, please?'

But one crisis averted soon made way for another.

'Cardiac arrest!' called Randall's houseman

urgently, as the boy's heart went into ventricular tachycardia.

The crash team went into action.

Drugs were drawn; injections given.

'He needs shocking! Everyone stand back!' ordered the medical registrar as he clamped the paddles on to the boy's bare chest.

They all waited while the boy's body was jerked upwards by the electrical current, and Kelly heaved a sigh of relief as she watched the monitor and saw the wavy erratic lines of ventricular tachycardia give way to a normal sinus rhythm.

Randall, who had been quiet, now spoke urgently to Damian, his houseman. 'This boy's bleeding internally. Can you ring Theatres? We're going to have to get him up there right *now*.'

'Right.'

'And ring ITU. Tell them we're going to need at least two beds. We hope,' Randall finished grimly.

Kelly did not know how long it took for everything to go back to normal. Patients were removed one by one, two to Theatres and one to the ward. The other lay cold and silent in the hospital morgue. Nurses began to clear away the debris—the bloodied sheets, the discarded needles, the empty syringes and used intravenous bags.

Tiredly Kelly made her way to the cloakroom where she scrubbed at her hands and her face, and tried to put the whole incident out of her mind.

It was easier said than done. One dead; one had almost died. The girl she had looked after had a badly broken leg and a wounded arm, but hopefully would recover. With Randall's case of internal bleeding, a sure diagnosis was never possible until the patient had been opened up in Theatre, assessed and then operated on.

She was just coming out of the cloakroom when she almost bumped into Harry, a grim look on his young face.

'I was waiting for you,' he said, without preamble.

'Why?'

'I wanted to—thank you. You didn't have to come in.'

Kelly shook her head. 'I'm glad that I could be of help.'

'Kelly,' he said slowly.

'What?'

'Can I ask you a—favour?'

'That depends on what it is.'

'Come here.' And he led her into an empty office, shutting the door firmly behind them and turning to face her once inside. 'That girl I certified, in the ambulance.' He swallowed. 'Her parents are waiting in the relatives' room.' He paused, and then it all seemed to come out in a rush. 'Kelly—can *you* tell them about their daughter?'

Kelly shook her head, her eyes bright. 'Don't ask me to do this for you, Harry. Please.

'*Please*,' he said starkly. 'I know what you're probably thinking—that I'm asking you because you're a woman, and that relatives take this news better from women. But it isn't that. I've never shirked anything like this before but, so help me, I can't tell them. Kelly, I just *can't*! I can't face them.

But you can. You didn't. . .have to. . .*see* her. . .'
He swallowed convulsively; he was actually shaking.
'But I did. And I don't want them to know—how—
what it was like,' he finished in a rush, almost in
tears.

Kelly dropped her head in her hands, understanding Harry's dilemma immediately. It was true, she
hadn't seen the girl; there would be no horror or
revulsion on her face. Nothing which would intensify
the grief of the parents even further. She knew, as
they all did, that it was well recognised that how bad
news was broken was tremendously important in
how relatives managed to come to terms with their
grief.

She nodded, her heart heavy, as she prepared for
the very worst that the job could throw at you. 'Very
well,' she said quietly. 'I'll go and do it.'

Kelly let herself into her room after midnight, glancing at Randall's door as she did so; but there was no
light beneath it, and she assumed that he was still in
Theatres, operating. Inside her room she immediately went to pour herself a small glass of brandy,
swallowing it in one, the fiery liquor bringing a little
warmth back into a body which felt frozen like ice.

It had been one of the worst experiences of her
life, to have to tell those parents—themselves still
only in their late thirties—that their only daughter,
their pride and joy, lay dead. All because a foolish
car journey in a high-performance vehicle which had
been stolen by the daughter's 'friend', had ended in
tragedy. The driver had been going hopelessly fast

down a narrow country lane. And, according to blood tests, he had been drinking. But of course Kelly had not told the parents *that*. Thankfully, that was not her task—that particularly onerous burden was left in the hands of the police.

Instead, in words which were heavy, carefully and painfully spoken, she tried to convey, in the best way she could and as she had been taught, that their daughter was never going to be coming home to them again.

Best? Derisively, she kicked off her shoes, not caring where they fell. How could *any* way of telling them be the *best* way? A young life snuffed out, and for nothing. Kelly thought that she would remember the terrible keening sound that the mother had made for the rest of her life.

By the time she had showered and got her hair dry it was late, and she yawned, looking at her watch to see, without surprise, that it was past one o'clock. She really ought to think about going to bed, and yet she needed to see Randall, quite badly.

She slithered into a pair of jade-green satin pyjamas, put some Chinese embroidered slippers on her feet, and padded along to his room. It still lay in darkness, but it was unlocked, and she remembered that he had left for A & E before her, and she had run out without thought of security in the face of a medical emergency.

He could be a minute; he could be an hour. She yawned again, before deciding that she might as well be comfortable while she waited for him. So she climbed into his bed and wriggled around a little, burying her nose in the pillow, like a dog hungry for its master's scent. And she *could* discern that particular heady, masculine aroma which was all Randall—soap and lemons, with some seductively musky undernote. A scent long-forgotten and tonight rediscovered in his arms.

Hurry up, Randall, she thought sleepily, but her lids were growing heavier and heavier. She would close them just for a minute. . .

When she woke it was starting to get light. The recognisably pale and cold light of dawn filtered through her still-closed lids, and she could hear a faint sound in the room. She opened her eyes by a slit, to see Randall standing over the sink, shaving, and that the sound had been the faint rasp of the razor over the dark shadow of his chin. He was wearing nothing but a pair of trousers, his chest bare. Through the mirror she could see the dark whorls of hair which grew there. His back was brown and broad and muscular and, oh, she could have lain in bed for a year just feasting her eyes on him.

'Hello,' he said, a smoky note of amusement in his voice.

She sat up, her mouth relaxing into a soft smile as she realised that the horror of the night was over; the new day was just beginning. 'How did you know I was awake?'

He turned round. The grey eyes were soft, the expression in them thrilling her to her very soul. 'I could tell—your breathing changed, almost imperceptibly, but I noticed. And in sleep your face goes very, very soft. Do you know that your eyelashes actually brush your cheeks, they're so long?' He said this as though it were the single most fascinating subject in the world.

'What time is it?'

'Five.'

Five! She had to be at work in an hour! 'And I have to be at work at six,' she said mournfully.

'I know.' He came to sit on the bed, but he kept his distance, she noted, and began to wonder if last night in his arms had in fact all been just a dream.

'What happened to your patient?'

He grimaced. 'He died on the table about two hours ago.'

'I'm so sorry,' she whispered.

'Yes.'

She suddenly felt a fool for being here; he had not touched her. 'What time did you get back?'

'At about three-thirty.'

Her cheeks went pink. He hadn't. . .got into bed with her?

'No, I didn't join you,' he said, with a tender smile, as though she had actually spoken her thoughts aloud to him. 'I've been watching you instead.'

'Watching me?'

'Uh-huh.'

After nine years, coyness was a slight waste of time. 'So you didn't want to get into bed with me?' She couldn't mask the disappointment in her face.

'Of course I did, you foolish woman—but what I *didn't* want was my damn bleep going off at a crucial moment after all this time! I've waited nine years for you, Kelly. I can wait a little longer. And we'll take just as long as you like.'

She couldn't think of anything worse!

She pushed the thick waves of dark red hair off her face. 'So what happens now?'

'You get up, because you're on duty any minute. I'm going to leave you to get dressed——' his eyes gave a rueful glint '—because I don't think I quite have the control to witness you doing *that* impassively. And tonight I'm taking you somewhere spectacular.'

'OK then,' she murmured demurely and pushed the bedclothes back, but she saw the dramatic darkening of his eyes as he watched the unmistakable outline of her breasts and long thighs beneath the jade satin which clung to every soft curve of her body.

'On second thoughts,' he said, in a voice which held the husky note of desire, 'come here.'

'Why?' she asked innocently.

'Why do you think?' he groaned, and pulled her on to his lap, his hands tangling in the rich cascade of auburn hair, before bending her head down to kiss him.

And the kiss obliterated every dark and dreadful thing, leaving her almost mindless with delight as he pushed her back down on the bed, coming to lie beside her.

They lay there for exquisite, timeless moments, kissing with such fervour, as though they were trying to make up for all the long years apart, until she was moving restlessly against him, aching with frustration, feeling from the tension in his body that he felt just the same.

'Shall we,' he murmured, 'get beneath the covers for a little while?'

'Yes,' she whispered, her heart racing out of control.

But once in bed, it seemed very difficult for Randall not to start undoing the buttons of her pyjamas, one by one, and stroking her breasts with a sweet skill which made her moan softly. And then he was sliding the pyjama bottoms off, and her hands seemed to be on the belt of his trousers, pulling frantically at the zip, until all their garments were kicked out of the bed, and he was naked and glorious and he moved to lie on top of her, his eyes dark as night with passion.

'You witch,' he groaned. 'You beautiful, tempting. . .' But the sentence was never completed because he had started to make love to her in a way which surpassed every dream she had ever had about him. And he did not need to finish the sentence for Kelly to understand, because she knew that—in his own delectable way—he had been telling her that he loved her. . .

CHAPTER EIGHT

'Darling! Wake up!'

It was a sexy voice, a deep voice. Through the mists of her heavenly dream, it sounded awfully like Randall's voice. Consciousness seeped back into her body and she came awake to find a pair of beautiful grey eyes looking down at her.

'Hello,' he said softly, and bent his head to kiss her.

'Hello,' she said, smiling—widely, foolishly, and idiotically most probably, but who cared? She felt the amazing, unfamiliar aching deep inside her, which somehow seemed to be what her body had been waiting for all her life.

'You've got about ten minutes to get yourself dressed and down in A & E,' he reminded her softly.

'*Hell*!' She kissed him quickly and jumped out of bed, hunting around the room for her pyjamas and beginning to scramble back into them.

He lay on his back, just watching her, his head resting in the cradle of his palms, his eyes narrowed with appreciation. 'You know,' he murmured, 'I think I shall always have to make you run late for work, if it means that you're going to run around the room naked like that.'

She threw him a look. 'I'll make you pay for that, Randall Seton!'

'I can hardly wait!' he laughed.

She reached for the door-handle. 'I must go.'

'Kelly?'

'Mmm?'

'What would you like to do tonight?'

She grinned. 'The same as you, I shouldn't doubt.'

He laughed again and she glowed inside at the richness of the sound. Heavens! Were all women as soppy as this when they fell in love?

'Bye,' she said softly, and opened the door.

'Oh, Kelly?'

She turned round. 'What?'

'Do you know how much I love you?'

She smiled, never as happy in her entire life as she was at that moment. 'I think I have a pretty good idea,' she whispered, soft colour stealing into her cheeks at the way he was looking at her. 'Since I feel exactly the same way. And now I'm going,' she said firmly, appalled at the way she wanted to do nothing more than go back to his arms and spend the day in bed with him.

She dressed in record time, and made it to A & E with seconds to spare, only to see Harry looking extremely surprised to see her there.

'I thought you'd be late,' he protested. 'I was quite prepared to cover for an extra couple of hours.' He paused. 'I owe you one, after last night.'

'Thanks very much for *telling* me that last night,' said Kelly ruefully, thinking that she *could* have spent, if not the day in bed with Randall, then at least an extra couple of hours.

She sipped the coffee which Harry handed to her,

her cheeks going pink as she remembered Randall's reaction when she had told him that there had been no other lover; that he was her first. He had gone very quiet, and said, 'I wish that you were mine.'

At which point she had whispered, 'Well, I don't. Because you probably wouldn't be so good at it.' And he had kissed her so deeply in answer to that. But afterwards she had not been able to stop herself from weeping a little bit, saddened by all the years they had been apart.

She was woken out of her daydream by the arrival of a male nurse who poked his head around the office door apologetically. 'There's a back injury in cubicle one,' he said, and Kelly immediately put her half drunk coffee on the table and followed him down the corridor.

The patient was a young man aged seventeen. He was lying flat on the trolley, his neck constricted by an orthopaedic brace, his brown eyes wide and worried.

Kelly went and bent over him, so that he could easily see her. 'Hello.' She smiled. 'What's your name?'

'Gary,' he replied. 'Gary Webber.'

'Well, Gary——' Kelly's fingers rested lightly on his pulse '—what have you been doing to yourself?'

He grimaced. 'We were playing with a frisbee— me and a few mates. It landed on the roof of our shed. I climbed up to get it down, and I sort of lost my footing, and slipped.'

'And how high was the shed, do you think?'

He said. 'Dunno. Twelve feet, maybe?'

Kelly nodded. 'And when you fell, did you hit your head?'

'Yeah. I put my hand out to save myself, but I caught the side of my head on the barbecue.'

'Did you lose consciousness?'

'No.'

'Good. And did anyone move you?'

'No. One of my mates said I should stay still until the ambulance arrived. So I did.'

Kelly smiled. 'Sounds as if you've got a very sensible mate, Gary.'

Kelly heard the fear in his voice as he asked the question. 'Am I going to be paralysed, Doctor?'

It was always one of the most difficult things to answer, especially before you had examined the patient. 'I don't know,' she replied honestly. 'We're going to have to do a few tests to find out what you've damaged.'

He winced. 'Can I have something for the pain?'

'Not yet,' said Kelly. 'We need to do some neurological observations first. Even though you didn't actually lose consciousness, we still have to be sure that there's no swelling in the head. Or indeed any fracture to the skull, so I'm going to order a skull X-ray to rule that out. You also need an X-ray to your spine.' Kelly took a pin from the pocket of her white coat and held it up. 'And I'm going to do a couple of tests of my own. I'm going to prick the sole of your foot with this pin. I want you to tell me whether you can feel it. OK?'

'OK.'

Kelly lifted the sheet and pricked his foot.

'Ouch! *Ouch*!'

She smiled. 'That's a good sign,' she remarked, as she then took the patella hammer from her pocket. She scraped the pointed end down the length of Gary's foot, pleased to see the big toe jerk upwards—a sign that there was no spinal damage, although not conclusive. An X-ray would be needed to confirm that.

Kelly scribbled out an X-ray form and handed it to the staff nurse, then bent over Gary again.

'We'll get you up to X-ray as soon as we can and, in the meantime, will you promise me that you'll continue to keep as still as possible?'

He gave her an engaging smile, encouraged by her gently confident manner. 'You bet!'

Kelly was just suturing an elderly man's head when the nurse informed her that Gary was back from X-ray, and Kelly grinned widely as she read the radiologist's report on the X-rays to his skull and spine.

She went into cubicle one, where Gary's mother and girlfriend were now seated on either side of the trolley, both looking extremely anxious. They glanced up as she walked in.

'Good news,' she told them straight away. 'You've sustained a hairline fracture to one of the vertebrae in your neck, Gary, but due to the quick thinking of your friend, by not moving you, there's been no damage done to your spinal cord.'

Gary's face broke out into a relieved smile. 'Does that mean I can go home, Doctor?'

Kelly shook her head. 'Oh, no. Sorry. You'll have

to be admitted. It's strict bed-rest for you, my lad, for at least a month, I'm afraid.'

Gary groaned.

Kelly smiled at his mother. 'The other good news is that his skull X-ray was fine——'

'You mean it showed that he's got nothing between his ears?' queried Mrs Webber acidly, and Kelly laughed as she bent over the trolley once more.

'Just one other thing, Gary,' she said, her wide mouth twitching into a smile.

'What's that, Doc?'

'Why don't you take up marbles next time?' And Kelly gave his hand a squeeze before going off to examine a child who had lodged a bead up his nostril.

His mother was babbling nervously.

'He knows never to put anything up his nose, *or* ear!'

'It happens more often than you think,' said Kelly. 'What's his name?'

'Luke.'

'Hello, Luke!' Kelly smiled down at the wide-eyed toddler, noting that his right nostril was running with slightly blood-stained mucus.

''Lo!' he answered cheekily.

'Been putting things up your nose?'

'Lucy's bead——'

'Lucy's his big sister,' explained his mother.

'Just the one bead, was it, Luke?'

'Yes. 'Cos Mummy shouted.'

'I'm not surprised!' laughed Kelly. 'Are you going to let me take it out now?'

He nodded. 'Luke brave boy!'

Kelly grinned. 'I can see that! Well, I promise to be very quick. Could you fetch me the nasal tray, please, Nurse?' The nurse disappeared and, putting her hand into the pocket of her white coat, Kelly took out a tiny, fluffy white teddy-bear, and held it out towards Luke. 'This is Harry,' she said. 'Once he got a bead stuck in *his* nose, so he knows what it feels like. Would you like to hold him for me?'

Luke nodded, and his plump little hand clutched the toy immediately.

When the nurse returned, Kelly dilated the nostril with some nasal prongs and, once she had located the bead, she slipped a slim pair of forceps up the nostril and withdrew the foreign body easily.

Luke's mother breathed a huge sigh of relief. 'Oh, *thank* you, Doctor! Thank you!'

'OK, Luke?' asked Kelly, as she pointed to the bright yellow bead which now lay in the kidney dish.

'Luke keep Harry!' he asserted, and hugged the teddy into his chest.

'*Luke*!' reprimanded his mother, but Kelly shook her head.

'Let him keep him,' she said, then lowered her voice. 'I keep a job lot of them for occasions just like this!'

The mother beamed. 'Got any of your own, Doctor?'

Kelly blinked. 'Sorry?'

'Kids! You're very good with them!'

'Oh, heavens, no—I'm not even married!' But to her horror, Kelly found herself blushing furiously, and she didn't dare stop to analyse why.

Life, she decided, had settled into a blissful, if somewhat erratic, pattern. She spent every moment she could with Randall, though these moments, frustratingly, proved not enough for either of them, since their duties often seemed to clash. Randall's senior registrar was on holiday for three weeks and, due to hospital economies, the management did not get a locum to replace him. Consequently, Randall's workload was about to be almost doubled.

So he reported back to Kelly, his face tight with anger, after a confrontation with Warren Booth in his office,

'Half of me wonders whether this isn't personal,' he told her, as the waiter poured them both a glass of Bardolino in the small Italian restaurant they had come to think of as 'theirs'.

Kelly paused in the act of chewing a bread stick. 'You're not serious?'

He shrugged. 'Aren't I? He knows we're seeing one another, and I don't think he's ever forgiven either of us. Believe me, Kelly, there's a way he has of staring at me with those pale, mean little eyes of his.' He shuddered. 'I really think he's a man with problems.'

'I'm sure you're imagining it,' said Kelly. But she remained slightly uneasy, wondering if there wasn't a kernel of truth in what Randall said.

And besides, she too had had her fair share of

hostility, because if Marianne Higgs had been rude
to her before she had started going out with Randall,
then she was now doubly worse. But the staff nurse
was very subtle, and her rudeness was never in front
of anyone else; indeed she was actively over-zealous
in being polite towards Kelly when they had an
audience. And Kelly didn't know how to cope with
it; she wasn't sure that the nursing officer would
believe her if she complained. After all, it was only
her word against Marianne's. And there was also
something defeatist about a female doctor complaining about a nurse, especially when none of the male
doctors had any complaints. Little whispers of
bitchiness tended to fly around the place.

She told Randall, of course, but he brushed off
her concern, in the same kind of way she had
brushed off his about Warren. 'You're only working
there for the next four months,' he pointed out,
quite reasonably. 'What harm can she possibly cause
you in that time?'

And, speaking of the next four months, Kelly still
hadn't fixed herself up with a job to go to for the
next part of her GP training scheme. That was
something else she intended to discuss with
Randall. . .that she was having second thoughts
about giving up surgery.

One night Randall was so busy on call that he did
not get to bed at all, and only managed to get back
to the room at six a.m., his face tired, dark shadows
beneath the grey eyes.

She woke up immediately, holding her arms open

to him, and he came over to the bed and gathered her in his arms, stifling a yawn as he did so.

'Thanks!' she teased. 'Are you bored with me already?'

His answer was to kiss her so thoroughly that she was left in no doubt whatsoever about his feelings for her!

'Come to bed,' she murmured huskily.

He shook his head regretfully. 'Can't. I'm due up in Theatre in ten minutes.'

'Damn!'

He gave her a hint of his devilish smile, but she could see how weary he was. 'Never mind. We'll go and have an early supper, then come back here and find something to do,' he finished, on a murmur.

Kelly gave a little grimace. 'We can't.'

'*Can't*?'

'I'm working. Remember?'

He said something very explicit beneath his breath, then sighed. 'No. I'd forgotten.' Then he gave a wry kind of smile. 'Do you know, someone really ought to do a bit of research into whether the birth-rate among married doctors is lower than that of the general populace.'

Kelly looked perplexed. 'Why?'

'Because they never get a chance to have sex together,' he said ruefully, as his bleep went off. 'That's me due in Theatre. See you sometime tomorrow, darling. Save me an hour, won't you?'

And during these snatched moments, they met each other's parents. It had been Randall's idea.

'Why?' Kelly asked stubbornly.

'Don't be dense, Kelly,' he teased. 'Because that's what one does when one is in love.'

'*One*?' she teased back.

She took him to the tiny terraced house in Hammersmith where she had grown up, casting him little glances as they walked hand in hand together up the dusty pavement, just daring him to make any kind of caustic comment.

But of course he didn't.

He was charming and courteous as he stepped into the best 'front' room, rarely used by the family, but opened up for Randall's visit, with the smell of furniture polish so strong that it was almost overpowering.

Randall demolished a whole plateful of egg and cress sandwiches, much to her mother's obvious delight, and then proceeded to do justice to the old-fashioned seed cake she had baked. They sat and rather stiltedly made small-talk until the arrival of Kelly's sister, Jo, who was clearly curious to meet Kelly's highly connected boyfriend. She came with her two small children, which immediately broke the ice, and the next hour was spent wiping noses and removing small china ornaments from their sticky fingers.

Randall—naturally—charmed both children, sitting them on a knee each and making up an outrageous story about the circus which had the two little boys giggling like mad. And when Kelly's father arrived, Randall accepted a glass of bitter with alacrity, and Kelly's mother even had a glass of sherry, so the whole affair ended most satisfactorily.

Until they got outside.

'You seemed to get on very well with them all,' said Kelly, as he unlocked the door of his car for her.

He caught her by the shoulders and gently turned her to face him. 'You don't sound very pleased about it,' he pointed out.

She hated herself for having the suspicion, but if you couldn't express your doubts and fears to the person you were in love with, then who else could you tell? 'You weren't—patronising them, were you?'

For a moment he looked extremely angry; a muscle worked in his faintly tanned cheek. 'No, Kelly, I was not,' he said quietly. 'And it rather sounds like *you* patronising me, if you have to ask questions like that.'

It was their first small disagreement, made worse by the fact that she was as nervous of meeting Randall's parents, who had agreed to see them on a flying visit on their way back from the Canary Islands.

Seton House looked magnificent in its autumn hues and when Kelly and Randall arrived there were two gardeners gathering up the fallen leaves. Against the sky she could see little puffs of smoke and the air held the smoky nostalgic tang of autumn, but more than that, Kelly felt as though she had been catapulted back into another age.

'It's such a different world,' she said in a low voice, but he heard her, and squeezed her hand tightly.

'I agree, darling. It is. But it isn't *our* world.'

But one day it would be, thought Kelly, as she went into the grand drawing-room to meet Arabella and Gideon Seton. One day Randall would inherit all this, and the house in France as well as the complex in New York.

Arabella Seton was blonde, ethereal and still beautiful, even though she was now in her late sixties. She had delicate bones and fine skin which was almost translucent. A thoroughbred of a woman, thought Kelly suddenly, feeling like a carthorse.

She looked Kelly up and down before giving her a glacial smile. 'Come and have some tea,' she said carelessly. Then, frowning, 'Do you ride?'

'No,' said Kelly stiffly. 'I'm afraid I don't.'

For a moment, Randall's parents both looked utterly shocked, as though Kelly had just admitted to some dark, dreadful secret. 'Oh, what a shame!' said Gideon Seton eventually, his ruddy complexion showing his own love of the outdoor life. 'Randall's quite brilliant in the saddle.'

Arabella patted the sofa beside her. 'Come and sit beside me, Kelly, and tell me all about yourself,' she said, then gave a delicate and perplexed little frown. 'Randall told me all about your people, but I don't believe I actually *know* them?'

It was torture; and as Kelly observed their cold demeanour she could scarcely believe how Randall had turned out to be such a gorgeously well-balanced man with parents like that.

Afterwards they drove home in Randall's sports

car in virtual silence, and it was not until they had parked at the hospital that he turned to her.

'Are you going to speak to me now?' he asked quietly.

'If you want,' she said, without looking at him.

'Kelly,' he said patiently.

She turned to face him, her green eyes dark and huge in the gloom of the car.

'What is it?' he persisted.

'Don't you know?' she demanded. 'Can't you guess?'

'It's my parents?' he hazarded.

'Yes, it's your parents! Or rather—it's not. It's me! They hate me!'

'They don't hate you; they hardly know you. It's just—'

'Just what, Randall?' she asked dangerously.

He sighed. 'You're just not what they expected, I suppose.'

'Or hoped for?'

'Probably not,' he agreed. 'But it isn't they who are in love with you; it isn't they who are asking you to marry them.'

'*What?*' she said disbelievingly.

'It's me,' he concluded softly.

'You want to get married?' she squeaked. 'To *me*?'

There was an unmistakable look of irritation on his face. 'Of course I want to marry you!' he exploded. 'Just what did you *think* was going to happen? For God's sake, Kelly, will you stop investing me with some of the qualities which my ancestors might have had! I am not exercising my *droit de seigneur*, you know—spending every spare minute of my time making love to you before dumping you in order to marry someone who's suitable! That is not,' he said grimly, 'what I am about. It has never been what I'm about and the sooner that you damned well accept that the better!'

She had never seen him so angry. They went to his room, where he almost ruthlessly took her clothes off and proceeded to make love to her with a skill which nearly had her weeping with pleasure, bringing her to the brink time and time again before he finally allowed her to collapse trembling into his arms. Afterwards, neither said anything, and Kelly stared at the ceiling thoughtfully for a long time after Randall had fallen asleep, bitterly ashamed because she knew that every word he had said was true.

He opened his eyes to find her studying him.

'What is it?' he asked.

'I'm sorry,' she whispered.

He shook his head and smiled. 'Don't be sorry, darling, just don't be silly. We love each other, that's all that matters.' He propped himself up on an elbow and looked down at her, smoothing back the thick waves of auburn hair from her forehead. 'You're tired,' he observed with a frown.

'Comes with the job,' she smiled, and with a gentle finger touched the skin beneath his eyes. 'And speaking of tiredness, what are these great shadows underneath your eyes? You're tired too.'

'Yes,' he yawned. 'I guess we ought to get some sleep, then?'

'I suppose so.'

But his hands were on her body, stroking her so that she moved ecstatically beneath his fingers, thrilled to the sweet plunder of his lips. Sleep was a long time in coming.

But over the next few weeks, their off-duties rarely seemed to coincide, and though they both tried very hard not to grumble about it, it put a strain on both of them.

One evening, Kelly was an hour from finishing duty when she had an emergency admission of a fourteen-year-old boy, whose GP was querying meningitis.

The boy was slightly dazed, but, other than that, showed none of the classic symptoms of meningitis, leading Kelly to believe that his GP was simply being over-cautious.

'Does your head ache?' Kelly asked him.

'God, yeah,' he muttered. 'Like hell.'

'Any neck stiffness?'

'No.'

'There's no sign of any rash on his trunk, and he doesn't seem to be at all photophobic,' observed Kelly to Joe as she shone her pencil torch in his eyes. 'Still, I'm going to get the medical reg down as soon as possible. He'll probably want to do a lumbar puncture anyway, to exclude——' But her sentence was never completed, for suddenly and without any warning, the boy collapsed and had a cardiac arrest.

Kelly pressed the emergency buzzer, and she and Joe immediately started resuscitation.

The crash team arrived, and they worked on the boy for an hour, but he was obviously very, very sick with septicaemia, and when at last they managed to transfer him up to ITU, there was very little hope that he would pull through.

Kelly could have wept with the unfairness of it, as she slowly made her way to Randall's room.

She sat down on the edge of the bed and kicked her shoes off, close to tears.

Minutes later in walked Randall. He came over and kissed her, his eyes taking in her pinched, pale expression. 'What's up?' he asked.

Kelly shrugged. 'Oh, just one of those awful, unrewarding days. You know.'

He sat down on the bed beside her. 'No, I don't know. Why don't you tell me about it?'

'Just that we had a fourteen-year-old sent in by his GP with some awfully vague symptoms. I didn't think there was much wrong with him at all—thought the GP was panicking. Then——' she let out a troubled sigh '—he went off—really quickly. One minute he was talking to me, and the next he'd arrested. We worked on him for an hour before we transferred him to ITU.'

'What was it?'

'Meningitis. The medical registrar had to tell the mother that there was only a twenty-per-cent chance of survival.'

'That's bad,' he murmured, his voice soft with sympathy.

She nodded. 'What's worse is that there's no follow-up, not for me anyway. That's one of the worst aspects about A & E. You treat people at the crisis point of their illness, and you never get to know what happens to them.'

'There's nothing to stop you ringing up ITU,' he pointed out.

'Do you think so?'

'Why not? He's your patient too.'

She thought about it. 'I'll ring tomorrow,' she decided. 'He's too close to crisis now, and the drugs will have had a chance to work by then.'

She hoped.

Randall was there the following day when she rang through to the unit and spoke to the sister in charge, and he didn't need to ask what the outcome was when he saw a smile like the sun coming up, lighting her exquisite face.

She put the phone down and hugged him.

'I gather that all is well?' he smiled.

She kissed him. 'Well, you know what they're like—cautious, but optimistic. But he's responding to the drugs they're giving him.'

Her worries abated, her attention was suddenly caught by the sight of a large cardboard box which was sitting on the floor underneath the window.

'What's that?' she enquired curiously.

He grinned. 'I thought you'd never ask!' And he walked over to pick it up, then handed it to her. 'Present.'

'For me?'

'That's right!'

Kelly looked up at him in bemusement. 'What is it?'

He smiled. 'To which he replies, "Why don't you open it and find out?"'

She took the top off. Inside were a pair of extremely sturdy brown leather boots. 'They're—er—lovely,' she ventured.

He laughed. 'Lovely they most definitely are *not*. What they are is functional.'

'And what are they for?'

'Walking.'

'Walking?'

'Mmm. There's a bank holiday next weekend. I thought I'd take you up to the Lake District.'

'Oh, Randall!' She threw her arms around his neck.

'Do I take it you're pleased?'

A long weekend alone with him, away from the hospital. It sounded like paradise. 'I can't wait,' she told him.

'Neither can I,' he agreed with a devilish glint in his eye, and slowly started to unbutton her shirt.

Marianne Higgs overheard them discussing their forthcoming trip the following day. Her blue eyes narrowed. 'The Lake District?' she asked. 'Whereabouts?'

She really was the nosiest girl, thought Kelly.

'Near Grasmere,' said Randall reluctantly.

Nurse Higgs tossed her splendid blonde head. '*Really*? Now that's a coincidence. My sister works at a hospital near Grasmere.'

Randall's eyes met Kelly's. 'I doubt we'll meet her,' he observed drily, 'since we aren't planning to go anywhere *near* a hospital.'

It was not until afterwards that Kelly was to remember those words, and be haunted by them. . .

CHAPTER SEVEN

I'M ABSOLUTELY *exhausted*!' Having just gingerly removed her sturdy walking shoes, Kelly collapsed back in the comfy sofa by the log fire which Randall was in the process of lighting.

'You look absolutely gorgeous,' he observed. 'Pink cheeks and sparkling eyes.'

'And I could eat a horse,' she said ruefully, idly reaching over to pull a red apple out of the bowl, and crunching into it. 'If you weren't such a slave driver, making me walk so far every day, I wouldn't be ploughing my way through such an enormous amount of food!' She sighed. Never had the prospect of returning to work seemed so gloomy. 'It's so heavenly here. I don't think I ever want to go back.'

The fire flared into life, and Randall sat back on his heels and watched her, the flames sending flickering shadows across his autocratic features. 'I know what you mean. I can't remember ever having enjoyed a holiday so much.'

They had been in the Lake District for three days, staying in the wonderful little cottage which Randall had rented. And it had been heaven. Days spent walking amidst some of the most beautiful scenery in the British Isles, and the evenings and nights spent making love. For the first time in her life, Kelly was actually dreading returning to work.

'It's hellish, us both being doctors, in a way,' she said suddenly. 'We'll never lead a completely normal life. You do know that, don't you?'

He shrugged. 'What's normal? Anyway, there's not a lot we can do about it.'

'I suppose not.' Kelly sighed again. 'Unless I give it up.'

He frowned as he came and joined her on the sofa.

'You're not serious?'

The thought of not having to do a twelve-hour shift suddenly seemed awfully appealing. 'Why shouldn't I be serious? A hell of a lot of people go part-time.'

'Not women like you,' he said firmly. 'And besides, why should you *want* to go part-time?'

She kissed the tip of his nose. 'Men can be so dense sometimes,' she sighed. 'I'm talking about if we *do* get married——'

'When, not if,' he corrected her. 'And why on earth should that make you give up working, even if we have a family? You can always fit your work in around it.'

Kelly thought of all the juggling; remembered the last female consultant she had met, telling her how impossible it was to keep all the balls in the air at once and that something always suffered. 'One of us will have to compromise—and it'll probably be me.'

'And how do you propose compromising?' he asked quietly.

'As I said. By being a half-time GP, I guess.'

'You'll never get the intellectual fulfilment you

need if you do that,' he pointed out. 'I thought so when you first told me you were switching from surgery, and I still think so.'

'Well, maybe there's more to life than intellectual fulfilment,' she objected.

'For some people, maybe; not for you.'

'Thanks for the vote of confidence.' She grinned at him and threw her apple-core into the fire with a perfect aim. 'It's just been great being with one another like this, rather than always having to snatch moments together. I don't relish going back to it. I—*ouch*!' She winced, her face whitening as her hand covered her abdomen.

Randall frowned. 'What is it?'

'Nothing. Just a pain. It's gone now.'

'Sure?'

She nodded.

'You shouldn't devour sour apples,' he teased.

'It wasn't; it was beautifully ripe,' she protested.

'Just like you,' he murmured, and pulled her into his arms.

But after they had made love, she felt odd—cold and trembly and then that sharp, bewildering pain stabbed again at her, but she did not tell Randall. There was little point in worrying him over what was probably nothing more than a touch of indigestion.

Randall cooked spaghetti for supper, but Kelly just picked lethargically at hers, and he saw her and frowned.

'So what happened to the gargantuan appetite you were boasting about earlier?'

'It's gone.' Her face felt pale; pinched.

'I can see that.' He laid his hand over hers, his eyes narrowed in concern. 'Darling, you are OK?'

She nodded. 'Of course I am.'

He sipped some wine, then put his head to one side and sat very still for a moment. 'How very odd.'

The pain had retreated. 'What is?'

'Listen,' he said softly.

Kelly blinked. 'To what? I can't hear anything.'

'Precisely. And what does that tell us?'

She gave him a rather wan smile. 'I give up!'

'Think what we've heard on other nights.'

No traffic drone, that was for sure. Perfect peace, apart from. . . 'The birds?' she guessed.

He nodded. 'Exactly. Remember we commented on how loud they sounded when they sang? But tonight there's nothing.'

'I'm the townie,' she smiled. 'I don't know if that's unusual or not.'

'Dramatically so,' said Randall quietly, and his voice had a quality of unease about it.

They were in bed when the storm started and Kelly never knew what woke her—the sound of the tree crashing to the ground in the garden of the cottage, or the pain in her abdomen which felt as though someone had ripped it open with a carving knife.

She opened her eyes to see Randall standing naked in front of the window, and became aware that there was a strange howling sound from outside the window, punctuated by another heavy thud of a falling tree. She wanted to get out and join him, but she realised that she could not move, the pain was so intense.

'Randall,' she croaked. 'What the hell is happening?'

'There's a storm outside and it's bad—very bad. I've never heard or seen anything like it in my life. We'd better sleep downstairs, darling. . .' He turned then, saw her face and was over by her side in seconds. 'Kelly? What on earth is wrong with you?'

She was trembling and sweating at the same time. 'I don't know. There's a pain—I, *oh*—Randall. . .'

He stripped the covers back. 'Easy, darling. Show me where.'

She let her hand vaguely brush at her side, then gripped her knees in an attempt not to cry out in pain.

With cool, expert fingers, Randall was carefully assessing and examining her.

With an effort she pushed her eyelids open, staring into his calm, impassive features. 'It's. . . appendicitis, isn't it?' she groaned.

'I'm afraid it looks that way.'

'Randall! What the hell are we going to *do*?' she wailed, for she knew that she would need an emergency operation which should not be delayed by a second if she were going to avoid the potentially life-threatening condition of peritonitis.

'You,' he said firmly, 'are going to be carried down on to the sofa, where you will stay and *not* worry. You will leave that to me, do you understand?' But his voice held some savage, grim note.

She felt weak; she felt helpless. 'Yes, Randall,'

she said, knowing that if anyone in the world could right this awful situation, then he could.

He carried her downstairs, and a nauseating wave of dizziness swept over her and she was sick while he laid a cool hand on her forehead, then, afterwards, he picked up the phone, his features not altering as he listened. 'The lines are down,' he said shortly, 'as I expected.'

'Then what can we do?' she whispered.

'We wait.' He saw her face. 'Just until we are certain that the storm has abated. Half an hour will make little difference,' he said. 'But if we go out into the eye of the storm, then we risk something falling on us. As soon as I'm satisfied it's as safe as it can be, then we get you in the car and drive you to the nearest hospital. And pray that the roads aren't blocked by fallen trees.'

'But what if the storm—what if it doesn't stop?'

'Then we have to take the risk,' he said grimly, and put his long fingers on her wild and fluttering pulse.

But the storm did abate; that uncanny howling eventually died down and the horrible creaking and thudding were gradually no more.

Randall wrapped her up in blankets and carried her to the car.

She had no idea how long the journey took, of how many times Randall had to slow the car right down. Her only reality was the pain; the pain which just got stronger and stronger until it seemed to dominate her whole world like some malevolent demon.

It seemed hours later when she heard Randall mutter something beneath his breath, and the car pulled up to a halt.

Blearily, Kelly opened her eyes to see a bright sign saying 'Scanton Cottage Hospital'.

'At least they've got power,' said Randall, still in that strained, savage voice. 'Darling—wait right there.'

'I'm not going anywhere!' she managed to joke, then clutched at her abdomen again as the pain returned with a vengeance.

He was back within seconds, lifting her gently from the car, and the grim tense look on his face filled her with some nameless dread. 'Is everything OK?' she whispered.

'It's going to have to be,' he answered obscurely.

Everything became a blur; the pain eclipsed everything. A nurse came forward; a nurse with a familiar-sounding accent. Kelly stared up into blue eyes and frowned, puzzled, but then the pain came back and swamped her confusion. The nurse dressed her in a hospital gown and then she and another nurse were pushing her down the corridor on a trolley.

'Where is the porter?' croaked Kelly.

'No porters on duty tonight,' said the nurse.

Kelly didn't understand. Of course there must be porters—how else would they get patients to and from Theatre? And then they were wheeling her into the anaesthetic room and a very old man was smiling down at her.

'Don't you worry about a thing, my dear,' he said. 'We'll soon have you better.'

She felt the scratch of the needle on her hand, and then she saw the tall figure dressed all in green come into the room. He must be the surgeon, she thought.

He was so tall. He had broad, powerful shoulders. He looked familiar. The drug began to steal over her senses as the tall figure walked towards the trolley.

'Count backwards from one hundred,' instructed the anaesthetist in his kindly voice.

'Ninety-nine, ninety-eight,' she mumbled, her mouth falling open and stopping in confusion as she stared above the mask into the grey eyes of the surgeon.

Those eyes. . .

But it *couldn't* be.

Because those were Randall's eyes!

It was the worst experience of his entire life.

An operation he had cut his teeth on, like all medical students, a simple appendicectomy he could have done in his sleep. He had performed countless operations during his surgical career, operations far more difficult than this, and yet he felt like a complete amateur about to tackle the most complex micro-surgery imaginable.

'Is everything all right, Mr Seton?' asked the gowned and masked nurse at his side.

'Yes,' he said tersely, as he pulled on the pair of size nine gloves she had opened for him.

He held his hand out for the scalpel which she slapped into his palm, glancing up at the anaesthetist as he received it. 'Are you happy with her?' he asked him.

The anaesthetist nodded. 'Ready when you are.'

Knife to skin. . .

Randall lifted the scalpel and the blade flashed beneath the bright glare of the theatre lights. He felt the cold beads of sweat forming on his forehead, and instantly the nurse dabbed them away.

He felt the unfamiliar tremor in his hand as he prepared to make the first incision, trying to put out of his mind the fact that the area of flesh lying exposed and waiting was not the anonymous flesh of an ordinary patient. That was *Kelly* who lay there, *Kelly* whose very life depended on his skill and his impartiality.

He swallowed once more as he brought the scalpel down to make the first incision. . .

Randall's eyes, thought Kelly disbelievingly, as she swam back to life from her drugged sleep.

She blinked as she looked up to see the tall, dark figure of Randall Seton standing by the edge of her hospital bed, staring down at her, an unfamiliar expression on his face. He looked, she thought suddenly—distant. So remote and aloof, not like Randall at all.

Gingerly she put her hand beneath the bedclothes and lightly touched the dressing which covered her operation site.

'How do you feel?' he asked. But it was his doctor voice.

'Sore.' And her patient voice.

He nodded. 'You would do; it was a nasty appendix.'

'You did the operation,' she said quietly, and he gave a silent nod, his grey eyes narrowing.

'Randall—*why*?'

'Because there was no duty surgeon and the nearest hospital was over thirty miles away. There wouldn't have been time to get you there, even if the roads hadn't been all blocked—which they were. As it was, the only person who was available to anaesthetise you was the retired anaesthetist who fortunately lives very close to the hospital. He was, by the way, quite superb.'

'I see,' she said, very quietly.

'You're under the care of another doctor now.' He paused. 'Kelly, I'm going to have to go back to London and leave you here to recover properly. Do you understand?'

'Of course I do.' What she *didn't* understand was why Randall hadn't touched her; hadn't kissed her; and why he was standing with that cool and dispassionate look on his face which made him seem like a total stranger.

'I'm arranging to have you flown home, when they discharge you.'

'There was no need for that,' she said politely, thinking that now they were even *talking* to each other like strangers.

'On the contrary,' he demurred. 'There's every need.'

He hesitated, as if he were about to say something, but when the word came out it only confirmed some niggling horrible fear which had just sprung to life in her heart. 'Goodbye, Kelly.'

She nodded. 'Goodbye, Randall.'

He was true to his word, and several days later Kelly was flown home on a private jet which Randall had hired, and taken by ambulance directly to her mother's house, where she was given her old bedroom.

She had not slept there for years, and it was very easy to cry herself to sleep, just as she had cried herself to sleep over him all those years ago. Because she knew without being told that it was all over between her and Randall. Something had died; she had seen that in his eyes the last time they had spoken, when he had stood over her hospital bed with that frosty remoteness on his face.

He did not come to visit her, not once, and Kelly was grateful for her mother's tactful lack of questioning as to why. She didn't know whether her miserable emotional state had anything to do with her slow rate of recovery, but it was a fortnight before she even *felt* like going back to work.

She left her parents' house and went back to the mess, where she bumped into Penny, her erstwhile squash partner who greeted her with the words, 'Are you better?'

'Much,' lied Kelly, not at all surprised by Penny's next words, but profoundly shocked by them, all the same.

'Why did Randall leave so suddenly?' asked Penny curiously. 'Do you know?'

Kelly swallowed, the word invading her mind like an enemy. '*Leave*?' She spoke the word carefully, like someone struggling with a foreign language, but she needed to be clear that Penny heard it correctly, so that she could deny ever having said it.

Penny nodded. 'Yes. It was the talk of the hospital for days. He suddenly upped and resigned—left immediately. Don't tell me that you didn't know?'

Sick with grief and betrayal, Kelly shook her head. 'No, I didn't know. We didn't discuss it.'

'Was it all—over—between you then?'

Kelly nodded, willing the tears to stay at bay. 'Yes. It was.'

'And he operated on you, didn't he?'

'Yes. He did. Now, will you please excuse me, Penny? I really must go and lie down.'

Pushed under her door was a letter. She recognised the distinctive black handwriting on the envelope immediately. Wishing that she had the strength of character to bin it, she ripped it open with trembling fingers.

And she had been wrong; it was not a letter. For the envelope contained nothing more than a few words written on a piece of writing paper.

It said, 'One day, I will explain everything, Randall.'

'Oh, no, you bloody well w-won't, Randall Seton,' said Kelly aloud as she painstakingly tore the piece of paper into dozens of tiny pieces and let them flutter like confetti into the bin.

CHAPTER EIGHT

KELLY glanced up at the video screen on the wall, and with great dexterity removed the gall-bladder through the sub-umbilical stab. Not for the first time in her career, she marvelled at all the great advances which surgery had made. 'Keyhole' surgery was fast and efficient, and left the patient with the tiniest of wounds, and she was one of its fiercest and most devoted fans.

'Thanks very much,' she smiled, as she completed the operation, glancing above her mask as one of the recovery nurses entered the operating theatre and approached the table.

'There's someone waiting to see you, Miss Hartley. A man. He's waiting in the staff-room.'

Kelly peeled off her surgical gloves and dropped them in the bin, then pulled the mask from her mouth and threw that away too.

'Any idea who?' she asked, as she left the operating theatre.

The nurse shook her head firmly. 'Sorry. He wouldn't give his name.'

'I hope it's not another drug rep?'

The nurse shook her head, then grinned. 'Oh, no. He certainly doesn't look like a drug rep.'

'Good. Well, would you tell him I'll be about ten minutes getting changed?'

'Yes, Miss Hartley.'

Kelly washed her hands, thoroughly exhausted but exhilarated all the same. Life as a surgical registrar took some beating! It had been a long list that afternoon, and what should have been a routine laparotomy had developed all kinds of problems but, thankfully, she had coped superbly.

Not for the first time, she marvelled at the dramatic upturn of her life and her fortunes, astonished at how satisfying she found her work these days.

In the two years since Randall had turned her life upside down by leaving her for the second time, she had worked, and worked hard, to achieve what had always been her life's greatest ambition. And she was now a surgeon, set on course for the top—or so her boss kept telling her!

And if the one drawback was that once more she had no one special in her life, she could only heave a huge sigh of relief. She had been down that road, and she knew now that she and love were totally incompatible. Or rather, she and men were. She had resigned herself to the fact that if she couldn't have Randall, then she did not want anyone. A one-man woman, that was her; it was just unfortunate that she had fallen for the wrong kind of man.

She had missed him, of course. In the early days, it had been absolute hell, trying to pretend that she did not want to hear from him, yet desolate when she didn't. But now the missing had become nothing more than the occasional poignant pang of regret.

Only once, early on, had she tried to find out where he was. She had been for supper with a pregnant girlfriend, and had drunk almost all of the bottle of wine they had shared. Egged on, she had telephoned Seton House and someone who sounded awfully like Mary, the cook, had answered. Swallowing her pride and knowing how much she was going to hate herself in the morning, Kelly asked if she knew where Randall was.

'Oh, *yes*, said the woman, and when she heard the familiar note of triumph in her voice, Kelly just *knew* it was Mary. 'Lord Rousay left for America almost a month ago. Was there any message?'

'No message,' Kelly had said tersely, replacing the receiver and breaking down in anguished tears.

Knowing that he had gone, there had seemed little point in pursuing her plan to go into general practice and so she had changed direction, channelling all her energy into her ambition, and managing to gain distinctions in both parts of her fellowship examination.

Going into the changing-room, Kelly quickly showered, then dressed in jeans and a silk shirt in softest coral. She brushed her hair vigorously, since the tight cap she had to wear all day to operate tended to flatten it. She had had her long hair cut to a more manageable shoulder-length, and it suited her. It was sleeker and more modern that the tumbling old style had been.

Snapping out the light, she walked slowly down towards the office, her thoughts miles away as she opened the door, when her startled eyes took in the tall, dark and elegant figure who stood facing her, the grave face still impossibly handsome. Like some betraying stranger, she felt her body stirring in response to the sight of him, and part of her wanted just to stand there and feast her eyes on him, like a starving man invited to make free at a banquet.

'Hello, Kelly,' came the deep, sonorous voice.

Her mind went into over-drive. She didn't want to hear what he had to say.

Did she?

She could go or she could stay. And half of her wanted just to run and run. But would running away not make him realise that he could still send her into a total spin, could still make her body ache and hunger for him, even after all he had done?

And what the other half of her wanted, she was horrified to discover, was very simple.

She wanted *him*.

It wasn't fair—it simply wasn't fair. She looked at him, lost in the silver-grey dazzle of his eyes, and realised that she wanted to find herself in his arms again, wanted his kiss, wanted him naked beside her, beneath her, covering her, filling her in the act of love.

She shuddered at her inherent lack of pride, determined that he would never know, and determined, too, to drive him away with a cool self-possession which would give him no hint of the turmoil of feelings he could still arouse in her.

'Hello, Randall,' she said coolly.

He gave her a long, slow appraisal, the silver-grey eyes telling her nothing whatsoever.

'I need to talk to you,' he said at last.

She managed to look faintly and superciliously

surprised. '*Really*?' she queried. 'I can hardly imagine why.'

A frown appeared between the dark brows. 'Yes, you can.'

She gave him a condescending glimmer of a smile, pleased to have angered him. 'Well, I'm not going to get into a slanging match,' she murmured. 'So whatever it is that you want to say, why don't you just get it over with?'

He shook his head, his gaze taking in the bleak office. 'Not here.'

'Then I'm afraid that I won't be able to hear it, because I don't intend going anywhere else with you. . .' She started to turn away, when he moved quickly to catch hold of her, and she felt the hot tide of colour ride into her cheeks as she felt his touch on her skin.

'Don't you?' he mocked her, and didn't even give her a chance to answer, because he kissed her.

For a split-second she fizzed with resentment, and then her body yielded to him as surely as a sapling bending to the demands of the north wind. And the hard, almost brutal assault of his mouth immediately became transmuted into something softer and infinitely sweeter as he gentled the kiss, his tongue licking sensually at her lips until she gave a little moan.

The sound of that helpless little moan brought with it the mind-jarring crash of reality. She tore herself out of his arms, her eyes slitted with anger and spitting with green fire.

'How dare you?' she whispered. 'How *dare* you?'

'Quite easily.' He threw her a mocking glance. 'I enjoyed it and so, quite obviously, did you.'

Frustration and rage combined to make her lose her temper completely. 'You think that it's the answer to everything, don't you, Randall? Sex! You think that all you need to do is to kiss me and you'll have me eating out of your hand? Well, you're wrong! Oh, I might unfortunately still find you attractive. You're a very good lover, as I'm sure you've been told countless times. But it isn't enough for me!'

'What isn't?' he said quietly.

'I told you!' she glowered at him bitterly. 'Sex!'

'But I wasn't offering you just sex,' he said. 'I never have done. I'm offering you marriage.'

She lifted her hand to slap him, then froze with it mid-way to his face, staring down at it in disbelief that she had been provoked to violence by him, she who had never laid a finger on another soul in her life. So these were the depths to which he could make her sink. . .

'Just go away, Randall,' she said tiredly. 'Please.'

'No. Not until you've listened to what I have to say.'

'I don't *want* to listen! I don't trust you any more! I don't want even to associate with someone who says things they don't mean. Someone who goes away, and. . .' She broke off, aware that she was on the brink of tears.

'I had to go away,' he said quietly.

She met his stare full on, her chin lifted proudly

in the air. 'And what was the excuse this time?' she
asked sarcastically. 'More concern about my career?'

He nodded. 'That was one reason. There were, in
fact, a number of reasons,' he told her.

Let him try and worm his way out of this one!
'Such as?'

He sighed. 'I'm trying to work out the best way to
tell you, Kelly. And it isn't easy.'

She felt indignant that he even had the *nerve* ever
to expect it to be easy! 'Oh, come *on*, Randall,' she
taunted. 'You've never been stuck for words before!'

'Sit down,' he said curtly, and pointed to a chair,
and then he added, quite gently, 'Please?'

His gentleness was her undoing, and she found
herself sitting without thinking, watching him warily
as he pulled over a chair and sat opposite her, just
feet away.

He gave a long sigh as he remembered. 'When I
arrived back here, leaving you in the Lake District,
I was asked to go straight away to the hospital
administrator's office.' His mouth twisted into a
savage line. 'Our old friend, Warren Booth,' he said
baldly.

Kelly blinked, then shuddered. Warren Booth.
Good heavens, it seemed such a long time since she
had heard her former boyfriend's name. And fortunately she had been spared the embarrassment of
seeing him, since he had left St Christopher's shortly
after Randall, under some sort of cloud, though she
never did find out exactly what it was all about.

'And what did he want?' she asked reluctantly,

her curiosity alerted by the serious expression on his face.

'He threatened to report me to the British Medical Council,' he said bluntly.

This was such a bizarre thing for him to say, that for the moment all Kelly's hostility towards Randall vanished. 'He did *what*?' she demanded incredulously. 'But *why*?'

'For operating on you.' His mouth thinned into a derisive line. 'He said that what I'd done was unprofessional, that I'd broken the laws of conduct, and that it was a flagrant abuse of power for a doctor to perform an operation on his girlfriend.'

'Good *grief*!' exclaimed Kelly in shock, as her mind tried to take in these astonishing facts. 'I don't *believe* it!'

He nodded. 'Oh, it's true all right.'

'But it isn't illegal to carry out an operation on a relative or a lover,' Kelly pointed out.

'Of course it isn't,' agreed Randall. 'But it can be open to legal action if it is thought that any impropriety has taken place. None had, of course, but that was the line of investigation which Warren was threatening to take.'

Kelly shook her head in bemusement. 'How did he find out that you'd operated on me?'

'You remember Marianne Higgs saying that her sister worked at a hospital in the Lakes?' he asked.

Kelly nodded speechlessly. Whatever next?

'Well, as fate would have it, it happened to be the one we ended up in that night. Marianne's sister actually happened to be the nurse who got you ready for Theatre; she even looked after you in the recovery room.'

Through the mists of memory, Kelly vaguely recalled seeing a pair of familiar-looking blue eyes.

'And she informed Marianne, who took it upon herself to let Warren know. It was a bit of a scoop to them both, since they were both bitter, Warren because of your relationship with me, and Marianne because I'd never taken her up on her numerous and frankly repugnant invitations to go out with her.'

What he had told her spun round and round in her head. 'But I would have died without that operation!' protested Kelly in a choked voice. 'We both know that!'

He nodded. 'Yes, we both know that,' he said quietly. 'And the road to the next hospital was blocked, so there certainly wouldn't have been the time or the means to transfer you to another hospital.'

She stared at him, not understanding. 'So why didn't you just fight it?'

'Because I didn't want to fight it. For a start, I didn't want to risk being suspended while it was all being investigated, or risk your career being affected by the accusation. And, yes, I would have won eventually, but mud sticks, Kelly,' he added quietly, if enough of it gets thrown about. I even spoke to a friend of mine on the Council, and he was the one who suggested that if I distanced myself from you for some time and let it all die down, then no one could say afterwards that there had been any kind of impropriety.'

Kelly had gone over and over that last dreadful meeting with him so often in her mind, that she could have repeated it word for word. Her eyes narrowed. 'But that day when you left me in the Lakes, when you came to see me—you were so cold, so distant. And that was before you say you were summoned to Warren's office. I felt that something had died between us.'

A look of regret clouded his eyes. 'And you were right, up to a point. Something between us had not died, but was in mortal danger,' he agreed. 'Which was another reason why I had to go away.'

Mortal danger? Kelly screwed her eyes up in confusion. 'I don't understand.'

He stared down at his long, surgeon's fingers for a moment, and when he looked up again, the grey eyes were rueful. 'It's just that the operation *had* changed something between us, and I was finding it very difficult to look on you as Kelly, the woman I loved and intended to marry. All I could see was the operation, playing over and over again in my mind. Of thinking that——' his voice shook a little '—that I was going to lose you. Of remembering what it felt like to actually *cut* you open with a scalpel,' he shuddered. 'And I didn't know if I'd ever be able to forget it,' he finished quietly.

Kelly nodded. 'I see. And were you—able to forget it? What am I now? Kelly the patient, or Kelly the woman?'

He smiled. 'You are Kelly, the living, breathing gorgeous woman whom I've missed with all my heart.'

And with these words, so honestly and beautifully spoken, Kelly felt the love which had never really gone away, burst into her her heart once more, and there was absolutely nothing she could do to stop it. 'Warren left shortly after you,' she said shrewdly. 'Did you have anything to do with that?'

'Not directly. But I let it be known that both you *and* I had had difficult dealings with him.' He saw her face. 'And, *no*, darling, I didn't go into details. I merely suggested that it might be an idea to keep a close eye on him. Which they obviously did. After all, someone who could use his position to achieve his own ends was obviously unstable. Not to mention what he'd tried to do to you,' he concluded grimly.

He leaned forward as though to take her hand, then paused, his eyes narrowing. 'But there was another reason for going too, even though on its own it wouldn't have been enough to make me leave.'

She nodded. She knew him so well that she had a pretty good idea what *that* was. 'Tell me,' she said softly.

'I felt there were still a number of issues we hadn't resolved. I could sense that you were regretting your decision to give up surgery and yet I also knew that you were reluctant to start on a course which would mean we had less hours together instead of more. It was your wish to be a surgeon battling against your wish to have a normal life. Ironically, I realised that all those years without you I had selflessly sacrificed——' he grinned '—to your career were about to be wasted, since you were considering chucking it all in just because we *were* in love. I remember that we spoke of compromise, and that you considered that you should be the one to have to make it, as women usually do. And I saw a way in which you wouldn't have to.'

She shook her head. 'I still don't understand,' she said, on a whisper.

'You will,' he promised. 'I suddenly realised that *I* could make the compromise. And that's what I set about doing. I've been in the States for the past two years, recruiting some of the finest research minds in medical science.'

She saw the passion and the commitment in his face, but she had absolutely no idea what was coming next.

'*Recruiting* them?' she echoed.

He nodded. 'I discovered that I had the answer to our dilemma. You may or may not know that I have a trust fund, set up for me by my grandfather when I was born. Piles of untouched money which I have no particular desire to spend, and which you've *certainly* got no interest in. So I've set up a research laboratory, which will be financed by my trust fund.'

'So you've just *given up* surgery?' she queried in disbelief. 'Just like that?'

He nodded and grinned.

'To administer a laboratory?'

He shook his head. 'No, Kelly, not to administer it. Someone else will do that. I intend to devote my time to pure research.'

'But what about surgery?'

'No.' He shook his head with determination. 'You

see, I've had my *own* career crisis, and I'm afraid that I've had it with surgery. The more I did it, the less rewarding I found it. I felt like a mechanic, in truth. I wanted to start using my *brain* for a change, instead of my hands. And I'll be working much more sympathetic hours than you'll be doing. Research hours are regular, so if we have a family, then I can contribute a lot of time to the children.'

Now this *was* a lot to take on board. Kelly blinked 'Seriously?'

He met her eyes. 'Why not?'

'There's the famous male ego, for a start,' she observed drily. 'Won't you worry about what people think?'

He shook his head. 'Why should I? I'm brilliant and rich and handsome enough not to give a stuff about how other people perceive me.'

'You arrogant so-and-so!' she scolded, but she was grinning all the same.

His face went suddenly serious. 'I mean it, Kelly. I want our children to have the kind of life which I never did. I want them to have us, and our time and I don't particularly care which of us provides the *most* time. I want to be a hands-on father. I don't want them sent off to boarding school at the age of eight, miserable as sin and missing us like hell. Do you undersatnd that?'

She nodded, swallowing a lump in her throat as she tried to imaging his sterile childhood. Her own might have been poor in the material sense, but at least there had been plenty of love around.

'I'm so fired up by the research,' he continued, his

voice vibrating with a passion and enthusiasm which was infinitely rare. And quite suddenly Kelly could easily imagine a future where Randall might make some discovery which would really *benefit* mankind, and she thrilled with incipient pride.

'I'm totally committed to it,' he finished quietly. 'And it's the second most important thing I've ever done in my life.'

She supposed that she was a fool for staring into those amazing grey eyes and asking, almost as though he was willing her to ask, 'And what's the most important thing?'

He gave her a soft smile. 'Why, not leaving here until you've agreed to be my wife.'

She looked at him. Wasn't trying to resist him the most pointless and stupid thing in the world? 'What would you do if I said no?'

He shrugged. 'I would persevere,' he said, in the distinctive deep voice. 'Using whatever means were available.'

Her heart beat a rapid tattoo. 'Such as?'

Had he moved his chair and pulled her to her feet without her noticing? Was that how she ended up in his arms, with his mouth searching hers? 'I've always found kissing pretty effective,' he murmured. 'Certainly with you.'

'Oh, really?'

'Mmm. Really.' And he proceeded to demonstrate with devastating effect.

She was out of breath and dismayed when he stopped. 'Oh!' she protested.

'One of your nurses just poked her head round

the door and looked extremely shocked, to say the least, but you were past noticing. I think, my darling, that we really ought to go somewhere a little more private.'

Kelly blushed. So much for her staunch reputation in Theatres of not being interested in men! Oh, lord, how she *wanted* him! 'I guess we should.'

He tilted her chin up to look at him. 'So will you marry me?'

'Yes, Randall,' she sighed in delight, wondering if she should change her name by deed-poll to Cinderella.

'And will you object to being Lady Rousay?'

She thought about it for a bit, then shook her head.

'Like you, I don't intend using it at work. But you've done so much for me that accepting the title is a small thing—and it might just please your parents.' It would certainly annoy them if she *refused* the title!

'Good. And are you free this Saturday?'

Her mind scanned over her off-duty rota. 'Er— yes. I am, actually. Why?'

'Because I just happen to have a special licence in my pocket and I thought we'd get married.'

'A—special—licence,' she repeated slowly, and he nodded.

Kelly's eyes widened. 'And how did you manage that?'

'Oh—I persuaded your mother to give me your birth certificate.'

'But you can't just *do* things like that!' she protested.

'I just did,' he pointed out, with a complete absence of modesty.

Kelly shook her head, and giggled. '*You*,' she told him firmly, 'are the most outrageous man I've ever met.'

'I am also the most patient, my darling, but not for much longer. So can we please leave now, before I'm tempted to give in to my baser instincts and have my wicked way with you right here?'

And when a man loved you enough to rearrange his whole career for you—his whole *life* for you—there was really only one thing you could say.

'I love you, Randall Seton.'

Temptation

Lost Loves

'Right Man...Wrong time'

All women are haunted by a lost love—a disastrous first romance, a brief affair, a marriage that failed.

A second chance with him...could change everything.

Lost Loves, a powerful, sizzling mini-series from Temptation starts in March 1995 with...

The Return of Caine O'Halloran
by JoAnn Ross

 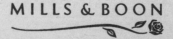

GET 4 BOOKS AND A MYSTERY GIFT

FREE

Return the coupon below and we'll send you 4 Love on Call novels absolutely FREE! We'll even pay the postage and packing for you.

We're making you this offer to introduce you to the benefits of Reader Service: FREE home delivery of brand-new Love on Call novels, at least a month before they are available in the shops, FREE gifts and a monthly Newsletter packed with information.

Accepting these FREE books places you under no obligation to buy, you may cancel at any time, even after receiving just your free shipment. Simply complete the coupon below and send it to:

HARLEQUIN MILLS & BOON, **FREEPOST**, PO BOX 70, CROYDON CR9 9EL.

NO STAMP NEEDED

Yes, please send me 4 Love on Call novels and a mystery gift as explained above. Please also reserve a subscription for me. If I decide to subscribe I shall receive 4 superb new titles every month for just £7.20* postage and packing free. I understand that I am under no obligation whatsoever. I may cancel or suspend my subscription at any time simply by writing to you, but the free books and gift will be mine to keep in any case. *I am over 18 years of age.*

1EP5D

Ms/Mrs/Miss/Mr _____

Address _____

_____

_____ Postcode _____

MAILING PREFERENCE SERVICE

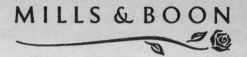

MILLS & BOON

LOVE CALL

The books for enjoyment this month are:

ANYONE CAN DREAM	Caroline Anderson
SECRETS TO KEEP	Josie Metcalfe
UNRULY HEART	Meredith Webber
CASUALTY OF PASSION	Sharon Wirdnam

Treats in store!

Watch next month for the following absorbing stories:

SMOOTH OPERATOR	Christine Adams
RIVALS FOR A SURGEON	Drusilla Douglas
A DAUNTING DIVERSION	Abigail Gordon
AN INDISPENSABLE WOMAN	Margaret Holt

Available from W.H. Smith, John Menzies, Volume One, Forbuoys,
Martins, Tesco, Asda, Safeway and other paperback stockists.

Readers in South Africa - write to:
IBS, Private Bag X3010, Randburg 2125.